THE SOUND OF MY VOICE

With an international reputation as a prize-winning novelist, Ron Butlin is a former Edinburgh Poet Laureate. Before becoming a writer he was a barnacle-scraper on Thames barges, a pop-song lyricist, a footman and a male model. He has published nearly twenty books; his work has won many prizes and been widely translated. His novel, *Ghost Moon*, was nominated for the international IMPAC Prize 2016. He lives in Edinburgh with his wife, the writer Regi Claire, and their dog.

ALSO BY RON BUTLIN

FICTION

The Tilting Room
Night Visits
Vivaldi and the Number 3
Belonging
No More Angels
Ghost Moon
Billionaires' Banquet
Steve & FranDan Take on the World

POETRY

The Wonnerfu Warld o John Milton
Stretto
Creatures Tamed by Cruelty
The Exquisite Instrument
Ragtime in Unfamiliar Bars
Histories of Desire
Without a Backward Glance
The Magicians of Edinburgh
The Magicians of Scotland
The Scottish Book of Rain

DRAMA AND OPERA

The Music Box
Blending In
We've Been Had
Sweet Dreams
Markheim
Faraway Pictures
Good Angel / Bad Angel
The Perfect Woman
The Money Man
Wedlock

CHILDREN'S

Here Come the Trolls!
Day of the Trolls!

THE SOUND OF MY VOICE

Ron Butlin

Polygon

This edition published in Great Britain in 2018 by
Polygon, an imprint of Birlinn Ltd.

West Newington House
10 Newington Road
Edinburgh
EH9 1QS

1

www.polygonbooks.co.uk

First published in 1987 by Canongate.

ISBN 978 1 84697 422 9
eBook ISBN 978 0 85790 998 5

British Library Cataloguing-in-Publication Data
A catalogue record for this book is available on request
from the British Library

Typeset in Verdigris MVB by Polygon
Printed in Great Britain by Clays Ltd, St Ives

To Regi

ACKNOWLEDGEMENT

The publisher is grateful to the *Village Voice Literary Supplement* for permission to reprint 'Great Scot' by Irvine Welsh as the foreword to this edition.

If you ask any student of Celtic literature to name the classic works of fiction originating from Scotland in the last twenty or so years, the list would be pretty predictable. It's a racing cert that Janice Galloway's *The Trick is to Keep Breathing*, William McIlvanney's *Docherty*, James Kelman's *The Bus Conductor Hines*, Alasdair Gray's *Lanark*, and Iain Banks' *The Wasp Factory* would all figure prominently. One book which probably won't be referenced by many people is a novel written by a Scottish poet called Ron Butlin, entitled *The Sound of My Voice*.

To my mind this book is one of the greatest pieces of fiction to come out of Britain in the 80s and I'm still a little astonished at the way it has been neglected.

Butlin's protagonist, Morris Magellan, is an executive who runs a biscuit company. He seems to embody the narrow vision of 80s-style success: good job, house in the suburbs, nice wife and kids, conformist lifestyle. In short, Morris seems on the surface to be an embodiment of Thatcherite values. However, there's one major problem: he is a chronic alcoholic, and, as we join his story, well on in the process of disintegration.

Unlike the New York- and London-based antiheroes of the yuppie novel, Morris does not emerge as a mere victim of 80s excess. There is no prospect of him chilling out a little, taking it easy, finding his level, perhaps redefining his life values. Morris isn't a coke-

and booze-bingeing style victim in Manhattan's Lower East Side or London's West End, with perhaps one eye on the clock, hoping to meet Ms Right and acquire the two kids and the suburban home that will straighten everything out.

He already has all this and it hasn't straightened out anything. That's what's so genuinely subversive about *The Sound of My Voice*: the way Butlin ruthlessly and skilfully subverts the cosy oedipal trajectory, that tiresome but omnipresent fictional journey where the hero slays his demons and marries the beautiful princess. From the start, we sense that the guy is doomed. So Morris becomes a far more terrifying ghost at the feast of 80s consumerism than your stock McInerney-Amis character could ever be.

The dissonant relationship between the central character's internal life and the external world with its harsh lights and sharp edges is best bridged by alcohol, what he calls his universal solvent. Butlin's book is a stylistic triumph, realising this relationship by utilising a second-person narrative that allows Morris's inner voice to maintain a clarity as his life increasingly disintegrates.

You had just begun to climb the stairs when you met her coming down.

A moment's pause, then you said, 'Hello, I was just coming to wake you. It's a lovely day outside.'

She stopped a few steps above you. She had already dressed, but she could only just have got up. Did she believe you? It wasn't really a lie,

anyway: it was a lovely day, and it would have
been a good idea to have woken her, to have
surprised her.

By adopting this device Butlin forces us to empathise
with Morris, insinuating the reader into the core of
his life, yet simultaneously, and strangely, producing
a sense of distance. It's as if the reader becomes the
central character, yet has no control over his actions.
This control, of course, rests with the drug. Butlin is too
disciplined a writer of prose fiction to indulge in crude
pseudo-psychological and sociological pontification as
to the cause of Morris's illness. His principal concern is
to arrive at an understanding of its nature through its
effects and his character's attempt to manage it. Yet the
skilful backdrop he paints affords us occasional glimpses
of a man whose mind is moving too quickly, sharply,
and restlessly for the banalities of bourgeois life, giving
everything far too much of a jagged, cutting focus.
The drug slows things down and smooths out the
rough edges.

Why was *The Sound of My Voice* not given its due credit
when it was first published? Well, it's decidedly not a
feel-good novel. More importantly, it went (and goes)
against the grain of the times in a quiet but ultimately
implacable and uncompromising way. Every age exerts
its cultural hegemony and Thatcherite Britain did this
more rigorously than most. Butlin's book was perhaps too
ahead of its time for the 80s; its unremitting, if implicit,
criticism of a spiritually vacuous, socially conformist
age is far more unsettling than many of the more

celebrated, overtly polemical works of fiction Scotland produced at this time.

As we move very tentatively forward from this era, I anticipate that *The Sound of My Voice* will receive the recognition it deserves as a major novel of its time and type.

Irvine Welsh, 2001

THE SOUND OF MY VOICE

You were at a party when your father died – and immediately you were told, a miracle happened. A real miracle. It didn't last, of course, but was convincing enough for a few moments. An hour later, you took a girl home and tried to make love to her. You held on to her as she pleaded with you: even now her distress is still the nearest you have come to feeling grief at your father's death. You are thirty-four years old; everything that has ever happened to you is still happening.

Whenever you were driven from the village in your father's car you would look out of the rear window to keep your house – a single-storey cottage – in sight for as long as you could. The road climbed a steep hill, and as more of the village, then the surrounding fields and woods, became visible, you strained to fix your eyes on the white walls of the cottage, trying not to blink nor look aside even for one second. There was never a point when the house actually disappeared, only the sudden realisation that it had just done so, as, for a second, though without meaning to, you relaxed your concentration and lost sight of it.

Later, as your father drove back down the hill on your return to the village, you began anxiously to check off each familiar landmark leading to your house: the manse, then the horse-field, the wooden barn. 'It might not be there, it might not be there,' you kept repeating under your breath. By the time you came level with Keir's orchard you had worked yourself into a state of almost unbearable uncertainty. Then, very slowly, you turned in the direction of your home. You prolonged this anxiety, this anguish, for as long as you could. It was, you knew, a measure of the joy that would come as soon as you glimpsed the white colour once more: your cottage at the foot of the hill.

When the car stopped you scrambled out. Your parents got the shopping from the boot, quite unaware of the miracle happening around them: you had left and had now returned to the very same place. Everything you knew about yourself was once more affirmed: your pleasure at making the unoiled gate screech; your fear of the dog in the next garden; your anticipation of going soon to gather the hens' eggs. In returning you home, your father had again restored you to yourself. You looked at the familiar surroundings, silently greeting each aspect of them in turn, then gazed at him in wonder and gratitude. He slammed the boot shut and went indoors.

One afternoon he took you and your mother for a picnic. He drove twenty miles into the Border hills, the windows wide open to let in a draught of fresh air. Every so often he had to stop to allow the radiator to cool. The first time he took off the cap you saw the boiling water shoot into the air. You thought it great fun.

'Will we get another fountain?' you asked hopefully each time the car stopped. You were three years old and still believed he would respond to you.

Eventually he took a small side road and climbed the

last mile or so to a disused farm. The car was parked in the yard and the three of you got out.

It was even hotter here and without a breath of wind. The snowcemmed walls of the abandoned buildings seemed themselves to be giving off heat. There were broken bricks and cobbles scattered across the yard like small hillocks, so overgrown were they with weeds and long grass. A harvester rusted in one corner, its paint flaked off at your touch; around it in the grass were several milk-churns, mostly on their sides. The windows and doors were broken, and it amused you to see small birds flying in and out of the house – one even perched on the window-frame for a few seconds and sang.

'That's his house now,' you told your parents, for when you approached him he flew into the room and stared at you from the mantelpiece as you looked in through the window.

It was dark and cool in the byre; there was a smell of hay and the roof had small chinks through which you could see sunlight and the sky. After a few minutes, however, you shivered. It felt chill suddenly, and you stepped back out into the yard.

At first you thought that the ruin and collapse of the farm must have happened all at once. You imagined that the farmer in a fit of terrible anger one day had smashed the windows, torn the doors from their hinges; you could picture him astride the roof, ripping up the tiles, then, standing at his full height, hurling them to shatter on the cobbles below. In fact, you were afraid that he might appear at any moment – and if he himself hadn't done all this, he might very well accuse you and your parents.

You were about to leave when you noticed a large trough set on the ground near the byre doorway. It was like a wash-hand basin, but almost big enough to be a bath. The water in it was filthy, with a greenish scum on top. Although you felt frightened of leaning over the basin, of placing yourself so close to the green slime, you reached forward to turn on the tap. The handle was very stiff.

You kept trying, but still it wouldn't turn. You used both hands and stood with your legs apart – your whole weight and strength concentrated on opening the tap. You could hear your mother shouting for you to come but you wouldn't give up, and kept tugging at the handle. Standing there in that hillside farm you could see across the entire valley; it was a clear summer's day. You shut your eyes to make an extra effort.

And suddenly it gave. The water gushed out at full force, splashing you, and giving you such a fright you stepped backwards – straight into your father.

'Will you come when you're told?' he said angrily, taking you by the shoulders. 'What are you playing at?'

'I—' you began.

But already he had turned away from you and was closing the tap. A small trickle was left running, however – you tried to point it out to him but he paid no attention.

'Can you not leave things alone?' he continued. 'Your mother's been calling you. Come on, we're going to have the picnic.'

Over by a gap in the yard wall stood your mother, dressed in a billowy summer frock. She had the picnic basket at her feet; she was waving, beckoning. She is dead now – and so is your father, but they were there with you in that farmyard over thirty years ago. You walked across the fields with your father at your left, your mother at your right. You had given them each a hand and were keeping up as best you could: three steps to your father's one, two steps to your mother's.

After a short walk you stopped on the slope of the hill. The rug was spread on the grass. Your mother unpacked the basket and then began laying out sandwiches, a tea-flask, lemonade and some fruit, while your father smoked a cigarette. The hill overlooked the main road, and after a few minutes you asked if you could go and play with the toy car and caravan parked in the layby below.

Your mother laughed, saying that it wasn't a model but big and full-sized. You didn't believe her – you could see quite clearly that it was no larger than your thumb-nail.

You got up and began running down the hill.

They shouted after you to come back, to watch the road. Even now, over thirty years later, you sometimes sense your father stumbling after you, still trying to catch up with you. So you ran faster.

The car and caravan are not far away now – and you can't wait to begin playing with them. The car is blue and the caravan is white with a step at the door. Almost there, you run with your hands stretched out in front.

The ground is levelling now – you are only a few

yards away when all at once the car and caravan become full-sized.

You stop in astonishment. Then you go back a few yards – and forwards again more slowly. Again they change size. A woman carrying a pail comes out of the caravan and, seeing you, halts on the step. She asks if you want anything.

You stare at her, then retreat until everything has become small again. You pause briefly before approaching once more. Then retreat. Back and forwards you blunder along this critical distance until, by the time your father arrives, you are nearly in tears. You are too distressed to speak.

Firstly, he goes and talks to the woman for a few moments; they glance over at you and laugh, then he takes your hand and leads you up the hill.

You looked back only once – everything had returned to being small again. At the picnic place you sat on the rug, lemonade in one hand and a sandwich in the other, staring down at the layby and trying to understand what had happened.

You ate and drank without enjoyment, staring straight ahead. Your mother, meanwhile, began a series of explanations – and although you didn't understand the meaning, you repeated the words she said inside yourself like a charm against your disappointment.

'Things far away from you seem smaller than they are – but really they are the same size all the time,' she told you, adding, 'just like that farm you were in. See.' She pointed back up the hill.

You turned round, knowing already what you were going to see. You had walked across the courtyard, stood in the barn and the byre; you had been hardly able to reach through the broken kitchen window – and yet there was the entire farm in the distance, as small as the car and caravan below.

'When I go away from here will I get smaller?' you asked.

Your father lit another cigarette and said that you were stupid.

'Will I?' you repeated anxiously after a moment.

'No, of course not,' your mother answered.

But *there* was the farm you had explored, where you had turned on the tap – a full-sized house, sheds, harvester, a large yard – now a model farm. The tap was still running, you remembered, and for some reason, knowing this made you feel very sad, desolate. You continued your picnic, and whenever the memory of your disappointment became unbearable, you repeated your mother's explanation, that charm, into yourself: 'Things far away from you seem smaller . . . '

Quite casually she then went on to tell you that the sun was really a thousand times bigger than the whole world – it looked small just because it was very far away, she remarked. After a few moments you asked: 'Do people ever go to the sun?'

'No,' came the reply, 'it's much too hot.'

So, you reasoned, the sun would always be far away and never get to its right size. Never. You were filled with a sense of injustice: some things would always get to be their right size, but the sun – never.

'It's not fair!' you cried out. 'It's not fair!'

At this your father laughed out loud, but you were so upset that you ignored him.

'How big is the world?' you asked after a few moments.

'As far as you can see,' he replied, 'and then there is always more. Go further and you'll always see more of it ahead of you.

'See that farm,' he pointed, 'if you went out through the front door and kept walking in a straight line for long enough, you'd walk in through the back door – now d'you understand?'

You could sense his pleasure in deliberately confusing you – but one thing at least seemed clear: 'There'll always be some bits that are far away then, and not their right size?' you asked.

He smoked his cigarette and said nothing.

You hesitated, then prompted him a moment later: 'Always?'

'Yes, always,' he replied abruptly.

If only, you thought to yourself, you could be everywhere at once so that nothing was ever far away but was its right size. Even for one moment.

Suddenly you remembered the running tap in the farmyard, and knew that when you went back to the car you would have an opportunity to turn it off. Also, it would be its right size when you were there.

A sense of joy began to fill you as you sat anticipating this. You gazed out beyond the road, across the Borders landscape as far as you could see. It was as if you had already turned off the tap, as if you had reached out and briefly were touching everything in sight – even the furthest hills.

However, during the thirty years since then you have learned to reason much better; these days, in fact, you rarely feel sadness or even the slightest disappointment. Soon you will be able to reason well enough to feel nothing at all.

Fear. Standing on the bottom step of the hall stairs while grasping on to the wooden banisters, 'frozen' as in a game of statues. Alert. Listening outside the lounge door, trying desperately to make out the tone of his voice or the quality of his silence, as though your life depended upon it. Which, of course, it did – and has done ever since. Terrified to enter the room he was in – and yet quite unable to go away.

You wanted to approach him where he sat in his armchair – just to say 'Hello' and perhaps touch the back of his hand lying on the armrest. But even to imagine *that* as having been an actual event in your childhood, if you thought about it now more than thirty years later, would make you catch your breath in fear.

Had he glanced at you, smiled and replied to your greeting; had that commonplace event ever happened, even once, it would have been the miracle to change your life. One moment of certainty that for all the years to come would have been yours to recall at will, saying to yourself: that was *me*.

Instead you spent your entire childhood in the corridor, as it were, knowing full well that if you dared to enter the room and address him or touch the back of his hand – if you dared, that is, to make the slightest demand upon him – he would ignore you. Or, at best, he would turn in your direction without speaking one word, his glance saying quite clearly: 'Well, and what could you possibly have to say to me?' Any affection you showed, he withdrew from. Any love you expressed, he crushed utterly.

One evening when you were in the kitchen cleaning your shoes for school the next day, he came into the room. You would have been about twelve years old and had long since learned to tense at his approach, but, as your back was towards him, you continued singing a sentimental pop song to yourself while brushing your shoes in time to keep the beat.

You have never forgotten the anger in his voice: 'What could you possibly know about love?' he shouted.

You turned to see him standing a few feet away, his arm pointing accusingly: 'I said, what could you know about love?'

His hand was trembling violently and his expression so full of rage that you had to look away. He repeated the word 'love' over and over again, with scorn, with disgust. Then he left.

Afterwards you remained standing at the kitchen window, holding your shoe in one hand and the brush with the polish still on it in the other. It was dark outside, pitch black. You felt, as you looked out into the night, that if all the darkness covering the village, the surrounding fields and woods, were taken into you, it would not be enough to hide the sense of guilt and shame that was there now.

But you were wrong. By your own efforts you have managed to keep these things hidden from the world – and from yourself. Quite forgetting their existence, in fact, until recently, when, while standing at a railway station on the way to work one morning, you were once again brought face to face with them. In that one moment the restraining force of over twenty years was suddenly released – tearing apart the darkness and yourself.

2

You'd decided to make a night of it, to get lushed and laid. At the first party you'd dived into the punch: gin, orange juice, wine, cider, plus some ethyl alcohol left over from what were described vaguely as 'Mike's experiments'.

'After three glasses of this you will be anybody's!' the hostess stated as she filled the glasses.

'I'm anybody's now!' you replied with a laugh. There was no sense of loss in your voice, not then – a Friday night all those years ago.

A party was a few paper cups, a towel wrapped around the pink bulb in the main room, loud music from speakers the size of bathtubs, three other people in the toilet and ash in the sauerkraut. The average was four parties a night – Friday and Saturday. Other people went to parties and got drunk, you got drunk and went to parties. There were bars like market places where addresses were swapped, routes planned – though, of course, if you heard Mick Jagger through an open window as you walked down the street, there was no harm in trying. Your father's death was announced at the third party that night.

Ring the bell so merrily, the two of you. I used to live here, you explain to the girl you'd met and brought along from party number two. Ring the bell again – the music's loud – and in you go. Hand in hand. Into a corridor of coats, rolled-up carpets and empty carry-out bags. Into the pink light and the boom-boom music. Boom in the stomach, boom in the groin.

'It's a *sine qua non*, of course,' says a man with a moustache. He looks at you, but seeing you are already with someone, he relaxes.

'A *sine qua non*,' he repeats, turning back to the girl beside him – her expression doesn't change.

'Somebody's locked themselves in the toilet – and Charlie here'll be throwing up any minute,' says a small man.

'Into the garden, Charlie, out the back window.' Good advice.

Charlie keeps leaning against the locked door, and the locked door keeps sliding from Charlie.

The girl – who's called Sandra, you remind yourself – is holding your hand. 'The kitchen,' you suggest, leading her past the boom-boom music, the *sine qua non* and Charlie. Across the slidy kitchen floor. Time to get the vital body fluids up to par.

'Something to drink?' you ask. 'It was like the Great Trek getting here!'

You make a joke about party-Boers, then slide towards the paper cups. Hello there, hello there, you greet the natives. They smile at you, then back away as if you were exerting some strange force upon them. They look at each other. White-man magic? you wonder to yourself.

'It's okay,' you explain to Sandra, 'they seem friendly enough.'

Helen, who lives here now, has put down her paper cup and is coming towards you. So is another friend of yours, Andy. From opposite sides of the room. They glance at each other, neither of them smiling.

It would not be hard for you to remember this. Not really. But you refuse even to try. Once upon a time you thought you knew and understood the ending: walking down a lane that gets narrower, and leads to your father sitting dead in his armchair. But now you have begun to suspect there is a great deal more to what happened, you would need to keep jumping to the end of the story – to the point where you walked Sandra home, then sat in her bedsit and began kissing her gently at first.

Helen and Andy are standing in front of you. The host and hostess. You introduce Sandra. 'We met on the way here.' You try the joke about the Great Trek and the party-Boers again, then continue: 'Looks like a good party.'

They don't smile back. A very white-faced Charlie slides past on his way to the back window.

'A *very* good party,' you repeat. You smile, and still they don't smile back.

Andy has taken your arm, and Sandra isn't beside you any more. The kitchen is suddenly emptier and bigger. Helen and Andy stand in front of you. For several seconds.

Then Andy says, 'Your father has died. Your mother couldn't get hold of you, and so she phoned here.' He grips your arm and asks if you are all right. Helen takes your other arm, and it feels as if they are going to frogmarch you down that narrowing lane towards your father sitting dead in his armchair.

Sandra was wearing white gloves which she didn't take

off even when you had arrived in her bedsit. You remarked upon this – stopping yourself just in time from asking her if she was going to perform magic tricks – then asked instead if there was anything to drink.

'On the shelf,' she replied. A small bottle of rum and some glasses.

She sat on the bed, still keeping on her coat; you went to sit beside her, putting the rum and two glasses on the small table. What should you have done now? Your father had just died. This girl, who you had met only a few hours ago, placed her hand on the back of yours. She did not look at you. She was biting her lip nervously.

'You can stay with us if you want,' Andy had suggested. Helen grips your arm again. 'Yes,' she says, 'stay with us. There's a back room; because you don't want to—'

But instead of answering, you're listening to the boom-boom music coming through from the hall. Girls would be dancing in the half-light, or standing at the edge of the floor—

A squeeze from Andy, and you're back again, being frogmarched down that lane towards your father. You can see that his head has slipped to one side against the wing of his armchair. Around him it is very dark.

The party is for Helen's twenty-first birthday, you remember now – and you have a present for her, a silk scarf, in your inside pocket. But because your host and hostess are comforting you – holding your arms at both sides – you cannot get at the small parcel. It would seem insensitive to shake yourself free of them. You begin to tell them not to worry: your father had been ill for some time, and his death is not really so unexpected. In fact, you add, it is a kind of release for him as he had been in considerable pain for some time. Lies, of course, but the tension eases a little, and so does their grip on your arm.

You try to raise your hand once more to get at the silk scarf. Immediately the lane narrows again, and you are brought close enough to see his slack mouth, his eyes staring straight ahead.

You cannot bear to look at him for long – sensing the measure of your own life in the distance between this dead man and yourself. Every moment is clamouring for your attention, even the briefest: the quality of that silence, for example, after you had given Sandra her glass of rum, the pause usually filled by proposing some kind of toast.

She was sitting at the edge of her bed with you, a complete stranger whose father had just died. She was still wearing her coat and gloves, and now at your suggestion she removed them. She had dressed carefully for a pleasant evening, and now she sat in silence. Before drinking the rum, as though to distract her from the unspoken toast, you turned over her hand very gently and lifted it to your lips to kiss the palm. Then you smiled at her, raised your glass and drank. She said nothing, but took a sip from her own.

'My ears are still buzzing,' you remarked. 'The music was much too loud.'

Sandra nodded in agreement. You gave her hand a slight squeeze.

'It's always too loud at parties,' she replied.

You were sitting close beside her. When you replaced

the glass on the small table you put your arm behind her, then gave her hand another slight squeeze.

'All right?' you asked.

She half-smiled, and so you put your arm on her shoulder to draw her towards you.

'He had a bad heart,' you explain to Helen and Andy. The unintended ambiguity of your remark allowed you to say exactly what you felt about your father.

'In a way,' you continue, elaborating what you have already said, 'it's a blessing. But even so, when it does . . . ' And you can tell by the way they are looking at you that they believe it all.

You add: 'I'll have a drink first and then go home.'

Andy begins to repeat his invitation to stay, but you are quite firm. You feel all right, you answer them – and anyway, you can't abandon Sandra.

'We can easily—' begins Helen.

'No,' you interrupt, and smile. 'It's okay.'

Then to settle matters you turn to go and get some wine. The miracle is about to happen.

You felt Sandra trembling as she sat beside you on the bed. She was eighteen years old, a first-year student, she had said. Into her small bedsit with the photographs of her parents, a Marc Bolan poster, and a teddy-bear propped against her pillow, you had brought the death of your father. You had made her the visitor in her own room. She sat on the edge of the bed, her head on your shoulder. You comforted her, speaking gently, stroking her hair, then her cheek. Gradually you turned her face upwards. She closed her eyes. You wanted to kiss her. Her cheek was wet. You kissed the warm dampness, letting your tongue briefly touch the salt-taste on her skin. Already you could feel the beginnings of an erection.

The boom-boom music is almost inside you now as you walk across the kitchen floor towards the drinks table. You know you are not drunk. You have just been told that your father has died. The room is steady and your mind very clear. You glance around for Sandra. She is standing by the cooker, isolated. You pick up two paper cups and move towards her. By the look on her face you realise she has already been told about your father.

'We'll have this and then go,' you say.

She doesn't reply, but looks at you uncertainly.

'Don't worry, I'll take you home,' you add.

There are still a few people in the kitchen, but no one else speaks to you. Everyone looks awkward – the sooner you leave the better. You raise the cup to your lips, quite unaware of the miracle about to take place.

You sip – and nothing happens. Nothing. No wine. You sip again – and again nothing happens. You tilt the cup right back – and still nothing comes out. You look into the cup – there is red wine, and the level has remained the same.

This, you realise suddenly, is grief. Your senses must be utterly disordered by the news of your father's death. You can see the wine three-quarters filling the cup, you can feel its weight – and yet, even when the cup is turned completely upside down, the wine still remains inside.

You hold it up to the light. There is no mistake: either the laws of gravity have ceased to work – or else you are so overwhelmed with shock that although you feel nothing, your senses have momentarily failed.

Andy is beside you again. He has gripped your arm and brought you face to face with your father at the end of the narrow lane, close enough to touch him. But, you reason to yourself while examining the cup, these scrambled senses, this miracle of the still wine that you are observing, must be simply the result of your own emotional delay.

How lucid, how clear your mind feels!

Sandra is standing beside you. She keeps her eyes lowered – maybe, you think to yourself, it would be better to take her home now. Andy and the others are looking at you, your arm raised to hold the cup up to the light.

'It's the wine,' you explain, 'it won't come out.'

You demonstrate, and if there is any trace of disappointment or confusion in your voice at this moment, it is because of this fact alone. Not grief at the death of your father – you are not referring to that as you turn to Andy, repeating, 'It won't come. See?' Again you turn the paper cup upside down, and sure enough, the wine remains in it.

After you had been holding Sandra for a minute or two and kissing her cheek, you began again to stroke her hair. Then, as you undid the top button on her blouse, you remembered the expression on her face as she had said 'Mine's the same' – and turned her cup of wine upside down as well.

The first and second buttons were undone easily. You began on the third while you kissed her neck, your tongue gently licking the skin. Your hand moved to stroke her breast. She caught her breath suddenly. Excited. Your erection was getting stronger. You kissed her tenderly while undoing the third button, so that you could touch her breasts.

'No, no,' she whispered. 'Please, no.'

You stopped briefly, then began once more to kiss her throat.

'No,' she repeated. 'I—' and again she caught her breath. 'No, no,' she was shaking her head slowly from side to side.

You continued kissing her throat. But more cautiously. The expression on her face came back to you again: 'Mine's the same,' she'd said as she turned her cup upside down and dipped her finger in it.

'Jelly!' she had cried out, laughing.

You had laughed too when you'd understood, laughed out loud, but now there was the scent of her skin, her warmth. Helen had been holding your arm to support you while Andy said 'Your father is dead', and everyone else could hear only the boom-boom music.

Sandra was beginning to grow afraid; she whispered, 'No, no—'

The sound of her voice was coming from further and further away as you unclasped her bra and began to lick the nipple erect. She tried to push you to one side, but you grasped her hand tightly, guided it and held it against your growing erection. The boom-boom music became loud enough to drown out the sound of her fear. 'See,' say Helen and Andy together as they force you down the narrowing road, 'See – your father's dead.' They make you stand in front of the crumpled broken-down body in the armchair. You were gathering into one moment all the years of his hatred and cruelty; you longed to push them so far into Sandra that—

'No, no,' she pleaded. But what could the sound of her voice matter now? Could anything ever cancel out the suffering you had known?

She was not wearing tights, so you pushed the crotch of her pants to one side and began to stroke her, repeating her name tenderly. You felt certain she would want to once you had begun to caress her – she was lying motionless. It was very quiet in her room. You looked up at her, but she turned her face away.

If only, you thought to yourself, you could manage to get your fingers inside her. You said her name again, but still she kept her face turned away; her body had stiffened. Cautiously you tried sliding your forefinger in – she caught her breath.

'That hurt,' she said.

The next few moments passed in silence.

Then with horror you realised that your erection had begun to slacken – you gritted your teeth and concentrated on stiffening the muscles while at the same time continuing to stroke her. The erection held, but only for as long as you could concentrate on it – a moment's inattention and it slackened a little more.

You had forgotten your father's death now. Of the

history of your pain there remained only this fast-weakening erection, this humiliation.

'I'm sorry,' you said.

For several moments the two of you remained without speaking. You could hear a small bedside clock ticking. Sandra's skirt was up above her waist; her bra and blouse were undone but she remained quite still.

'Perhaps I'd better go,' you said as you got up from the bed. She did not reply.

'Listen,' you began again, 'I'm very sorry for all this. It's not been—' But you couldn't continue.

She sat up, straightened her skirt, buttoned her blouse, then watched as you went to the back of the chair to pick up your coat.

'Don't let's part like this,' you said as you went towards the door. 'Not like this, when it could have—'

'Why *not* part like this?' she demanded with sudden anger.

She stood up, crossed the room, and opened the door.

'Sandra . . . '

'Well?'

'Well, I . . . ' But you didn't know what to say.

'Well?' she insisted.

Somewhere in the building a lift shuddered. She was waiting for you to speak. Over her shoulder you could see the crumpled bed, and on the small side table the rum and the two empty glasses. What did you want to say? What could you say?

'I . . . ' you began again.

'Yes?' Her voice was no longer so angry. She looked at you as she held the door open.

'I . . .' you repeated, but again you could get no further. You bit your lip. If she had laid her hand on your arm at that moment, as Andy and Helen had done earlier, you would probably have burst into tears. By yourself, however, you could do nothing.

Instead you pointed beyond her into the room. You were trying very hard to speak.

'It's not like *this*,' you managed to say eventually, and then stopped. You pointed with one hand, the other clenched at your side.

'It's not like this,' you repeated.

You could hardly believe the effort it was taking to say even these words.

'Not like this – not now,' you faltered.

You looked into her face. A complete stranger: a girl with a blonde fringe, eye-shadow, a yellow blouse.

'This,' you continued, indicating the crumpled bed, the rum.

You seemed about to take a step into the room, but didn't. Your fist clenched tighter.

'Sandra, I need . . . I need—' you tried again, but stopped.

If everything you had ever longed for had been set before you at that moment, you would have swept it aside in despair, in disgust even.

'Yes?' she answered.

You had taken her hand, and were no longer looking at her. After a short pause you heard her repeat the word

'Yes?' Then she placed her other hand on yours. You were trembling.

For several moments the two of you stood like that without speaking, then the lift shuddered again. You listened to it until it came to a standstill.

'I'd better go,' you said.

Sandra nodded.

'Goodbye,' you said, then paused, uncertain whether to kiss her, shake hands perhaps.

'Goodbye,' she said.

You turned – and when you reached the end of the corridor you looked back to see if she was still there. But already you had seen her for the last time.

It was nearly dawn when you arrived at your flat after walking through the deserted streets. You climbed the stairs, opened the door, and went in. You expected to be afraid, to sense your father's presence – and so you looked into each of the rooms in turn before going to bed. After a short but deep sleep, you took the train home the following morning.

Since then, however, you have felt demons inside you, dancing to the boom-boom music. They lead you down a narrowing lane. Death, they tell you, is simply a failure to see far enough into the darkness. Recently their tempo has quickened. You have tried to keep pace with them, learning that Time is a straight line only to those needing to prove themselves sober. Each moment has become the sound of Sandra's voice pitched between anger and compassion; it is the quickening rhythm of the boom-boom music. For you, there is the fear of immortality in the pause between drinks.

3

You are thirty-four years old and already two-thirds destroyed. When your friends and business colleagues meet you they shake your hand and say, 'Hello, Morris.' You reply, 'Hello,' usually smiling. At home your wife and children – your accusations, as you call them – love you and need you. You know all this, and know that it is not enough.

Every day, every moment almost, you must begin the struggle over again – the struggle to be yourself. You keep trying, like an actor learning his lines, in the belief that eventually, if you work hard enough, you will play the part of 'Morris Magellan' convincingly. In time you hope to convince even yourself.

Over the years you have become very skilful at sensing what is expected of you, irrespective of your own needs or wishes. You have never been accepted, nor have you ever tried to be; *you* have never loved, hated or been angry. Instead you have known only the anxieties of performance: that you do not make even one mistake by forgetting a line or missing a cue.

There are two histories to your life: one that belongs to other people – this history has many variations – and another that is yours alone. Both of them are true: their contradictions must be maintained and resolved inside you every moment of your life. In effect, you carry the burden of two lives at least, and not only are you running out of energy to do this, but you realise you have lost sight of any purpose to this weary exercise.

In the conventional script there has to be a leading lady. Nowadays she is played by Mary, but there have been others – from those you attempted to coach into the role by flattery, manipulation, pleasing, or whatever seemed required over a course of weeks, months or years, to last-minute understudies who were forgotten the morning after. You needed to have someone to speak her lines in answer to yours, to respond to your gestures – someone who played her part well enough that the show could go on.

When you discovered a leading lady with whom the script seemed to make sense, you called this *love*. And when you said you loved her you looked into her eyes with such hope – hope that she would not stumble over her reply nor embarrass you with a silence. For nothing can erase the silence or even slightest hesitation that one day answers the words, 'I love you.' Sensing there was awkwardness to come, a lesser actor would have ignored everything and insisted on speaking lines already grown more and more ridiculous. You, the greater actor, raised yourself above deception: your declarations of love would sound convincing right until the last moment. What a flawless performance you have learnt to give over the years.

Exit one leading lady and enter her replacement – your main concern was not to confuse their stage names. That way you felt you knew what you were doing. As though a sailor – you are called 'Magellan' after all – could expect to control the sea-weather by renaming his ship whenever a storm threatened! You believed that the intensity, the conviction, with which you loved could save you – as though a drowning man could save himself simply by an effort of will! Each time you fell in love you tried harder, and more desperately. So many histories, so many performances of the same play – and you, trying to make everything appear real and true at all times, trying to overcome a worn-out plot with passion and pretence. The effort has almost killed you.

The downstairs clock had just struck four. Having woken up, you couldn't get back to sleep. Mary lay beside you, breathing very gently. The alarm clock ticked busily. Though you had been asleep for three hours you were still rather drunk, but at least the room had settled down since you saw it last: the floor was less storm-tossed, the walls no longer billowing in and out like sails.

Mary must have taken off your jacket and shoes before putting the top blanket over you. An understanding woman. A night out for the biscuit-men and their wives – could anyone have endured that sober? Not that many seemed to be trying. You needed to be drunk to feel normal with all those publicity-biscuits walking round in high heels, cardboard and tassels. The launching of a new line: British biscuits – famous historical characters covered in chocolate, and each with its own particular flavour. Wrapped in Union Jack foil. Patriotic. Educational.

No wonder you had felt sick – a Newton, two Shakespeares, a Nell Gwyn, a Drake and a Margaret Thatcher. But no one seemed to notice.

After a short sleep you were feeling better and could move your head without bending the room in the same direction. The bed was horizontal.

'Like being on board a ship,' you had remarked to Mary as the two of you crossed the hall.

'Sea-legs?' she enquired.

You tried to keep hold of the banisters, the stairs rolling and pitching beneath your feet.

'A bit stormy here,' you called out as you rounded the landing.

Eventually you reached the bedroom.

'Our harbour and haven,' you insisted. 'Not the dry dock.'

You intended having grog rations issued immediately, but once you had lain down on the bed the slightest movement made the walls and ceiling ripple uneasily. You lay trembling like a compass needle about to settle. By concentrating hard you steadied everything, briefly. The moment your concentration slackened, however, the room began sliding sideways once more. You kept your eyes wide open to hold the ceiling in place. You had to keep concentrating. It was a comfort to know that very soon you would pass out.

When Mary got into bed you felt the room slip momentarily from your grasp. You let it go.

It returned. Lopsidedly.

Then, like a television picture with the horizontal

hold gone, it began to flip over and over and over ...

That had been a few hours earlier. No hangover – but four in the morning is always a very deceptive time: the head is still drying out and things could yet go either way.

You have been a loyal biscuit-man for many years, having worked your way out of the open-plan and into a private office. You are one of the few executives who consume a Majestic biscuit occasionally, but that night's complete pack of six of the 'Best of British' was beyond the call of duty. You exceeded your office, let's say – usually you just drink there with Bach, Beethoven, Mozart or whoever. You never drink alone. By noon, especially if it's a high and dry noon, things often become a little scrambled, pulling you this way and that, and work becomes impossible until you've relocated your position. Its co-ordinates, as you discovered some time ago, are the taste of brandy and the sound of a Mozart string quartet. Whenever possible, lunchtime and at least part of the afternoon are spent in trying your hardest to remain on course. The more you drink, the more easily you can distinguish between north, south, east and west. By five o'clock you have usually drunk enough to find your way home.

That night, however, it had been hard enough finding your way upstairs to bed. Even with Mary to navigate.

It was almost light now. Another Sunday: the shortest day of the week when compared with those in your weekday biscuit-tin box, but, close to, the most wearying of them all. The accusations would need attention, the house, the garden, the car would all need attention – and so would Mary.

It used to be the case that each time you fell in love, the effort of loving released in you the energy to hold everything together a little longer. Then, after several months or years, when things began to crack apart again, you would fall in love with someone else. New energy would be released, and for a time you and your world would be safe once more.

By now, however, you have exhausted that. There seems to be no energy left – if you had discovered alcohol earlier it might have saved a few broken hearts. For you, alcohol is not the problem – it's the solution: dissolving all the separate parts into one. A universal solvent. An ocean.

Thirty-four years ago you were born in a small ocean and came into the world on its fullest tide, washed ashore after many months drifting hopelessly at sea. These days, however, you live from moment to moment like a drowning man. When you drink you cease struggling and slip gradually below the surface, easing yourself down fathom by fathom. Six feet at a time; burial at sea. Letting the turbulent waters close far above you, you sink to a gentle rest upon the seabed. There, nothing can touch or hurt you. All movement is slowed down, all noise silenced. Anxiety and even anger are no more than gentle disturbances in the atmosphere, caresses almost, ebbing back and forth.

The moments in your life you regard as the divisions on a compass rather than on a clock face: there are no dates and numbers, but directions, possibilities whose 'longevity' depends upon your commitment to what is happening, i.e. upon how drunk you are. Time is the sense of longing you feel to be elsewhere.

At first you wanted to drink the ocean dry, but as you did so all manner of horrors – both living and dead – were exposed. These creatures groped sightlessly towards you. The more horrific they were, the more you drank – as though trying to swallow them, to remove them from sight. You don't drink to forget – it doesn't happen that way any more – instead, the ocean has become everything that has ever happened to you, and when you drink you can swim effortlessly wherever the mood suggests. You do drink like a fish, for drink allows you to breathe underwater.

No one likes it when you go down to the ocean by yourself. They don't like that at all. Nor when you turn politely to look back at them from the other side of a dinner table, for example, then wave goodbye as you sink smoothly out of sight. Occasionally, guests have arrived to find you already waterlogged, let's say, and beached comfortably on the lounge carpet. Such drinking is what your wife, who understands these matters, would call 'displaced activity'. Displaced in the liquid of your own choice!

Mary is very understanding. In fact, she understands your problems much better than you do – and works harder at them. Whenever there is a summit conference to deal with the latest crisis in your life, she asks all the questions and gives all the answers. You are required simply to nod: it is enough that you have provided the agenda for discussion. Your relationship with her reads like a very scholarly book: each page has two or three lines of actual text at the top, your contribution; the remaining nine-tenths of the page is her commentary and footnotes in the smallest, most discreet print possible.

A few days before, you had thrown a wine bottle against the kitchen wall. Instead of getting down on her hands and knees to clear up the broken glass, she immediately put her arms around you and assured you how unhappy you must feel. Hardly news. When she added that you were killing yourself – well, that was hardly news either. In fact, it was more like an acknowledgement of your method, a sort of encouragement. Only after you'd threatened to hit her with the next bottle did she become a little less understanding.

Saturday had been a big biscuit day: Majestic Baking Co. Ltd, morning, noon and night. Your business is biscuits – the new 'Best of British' among others. 480 per minute. Early that evening you came home to change and not-to-drink before the reception. The latter was your own idea, but inspired, let's say, by others.

You had passed the afternoon in your third-floor office of a west-facing biscuit tin. You kept your window open; the sky was a cloudless haze unmarked even by the sun; pure brightness. The air was so heavy and still that, being hardly able to breathe, you felt you were drowning fathoms deep in an invisible ocean. All around was so much debris – the cars, lorries, the other vast biscuit tins – that had drifted down at some former time and settled on the muddy sea-bed. Above, you could see the waters standing clear and untroubled.

But in your office, in your third-floor mud-trap, your hands left sweatmarks wherever you touched. By three o'clock you needed a few minutes away from the administration of biscuits; you needed to look up from your desk and gaze at the ocean, to cleanse yourself in its invisible, immaculate waters. Also, you needed brandy and Schubert's 'Unfinished'.

And so: round with the executive swivel, feet up on the sill, the brandy handy and yourself plugged in. At 480 Majestics a minute, Schubert weighed in at approx. 9,500 biscuits.

No matter how clean and fresh the day appears, soon enough mud starts seeping in. After some brandy and Schubert, some brandy and Bach. You could tell from a glance at the mud-skies and mud-streets that it was getting towards late afternoon. In a short time you would be on a train hardly able to push its way along the rails, a train having to struggle free of each station. After six stops you would heave yourself up from your seat, ease yourself on to the platform, then wade home.

Mud-streets, mud-skies, and – inside you – the mud rising. You drink to keep it down, to stop from choking. You drink to gain another breath – and so you struggled through the afternoon. Recently it has been getting hard for you to struggle through the morning as well. Sometimes you wake already choking in mud. But not always, not yet.

In a few minutes it would be the dawn of a beautiful summer's day. Sunday. Clean, clear colours with a sense of space. Very faint light was coming through a gap in the curtains. You could see Mary beside you, outlined in shadows and blanket-folds. A good sleeper, a natural.

You had had a shower as soon as you had returned home from the mud-trap, then changed into the informal suit and shoes. Mary was in the bedroom preparing for the biscuit soirée. She had chosen green earrings, a sea-green that brought out a colour in her eyes you had not seen for a long time. She was sitting at her dressing table, her head tilted slightly to one side as she fastened the clasp.

A few heavy drops had begun falling as you came along the street, and now you could hear the downpour that followed rumbles of thunder. A wind had started up after the sultry day, and every few moments rain smashed against the window. Mary had not heard you enter the room. For several seconds you considered the image of her face in one of the side-mirrors, the old-fashioned dressing table having a set of the triptych variety. She was humming to herself as she fixed the earring in place.

Were you aware of how much it disturbed you to watch her putting the finishing touches to her make-up? It lasted only a few minutes, yet during that time you could feel mud from the ocean floor being stirred up inside you.

She leant closer to the glass to apply the eye-shadow, looking critically, then rubbing carefully with the tip of her finger until the effect pleased her. She smiled to herself, picked up the lipstick, and very delicately applied a faint red to her lips.

You watched, standing by the doorway; you felt excluded and even jealous, perhaps, of this intimacy she had with her appearance. Whatever, you could not remain a witness to it much longer – either you had to withdraw or else go up to her and, most likely, pay her a compliment, then kiss her bare shoulder. The mud was rising inside you, filling your chest until you could hardly breathe, and yet you didn't move.

She was giving her hair a final, smoothing touch with a comb, almost a caress it seemed to you, when suddenly she started back – then laughed.

'I didn't see you there!' she exclaimed, then smiled at you in the mirror. But as she spoke you could see her face already strained with the effort of making that smile and its reassurance. You went up and stood behind her; your eyes met hers in the mirror.

'You look very lovely,' you complimented her, then bent to kiss her bare shoulder.

'Thank you,' she replied.

You turned and went over to the window. Though it was hardly seven o'clock, darkness seemed to have already fallen. The rain was even heavier.

'I suppose they'll hold it indoors?' she asked.

'They'll have to – no one likes soggy biscuits!'

The side-light by which Mary was seeing to get ready was reflected in the window-pane – and so, rather than the street outside, you saw the image of the bedroom behind you detailed on the glass. She had stopped what she was doing and was looking in your direction. You thought you had managed to present yourself well, but the expression on her face – now that your back was turned – was one of pity. You paused for a moment, then turned away from her image to face her directly.

Pity, you thought to yourself. The more bottles you threw at the wall, the more she would overwhelm you with pity. Probably if you did break a bottle over her head, her dying glance would say, 'I pity you, I pity you.' Pity. The word is pronounced like the act of spitting.

'Your tie's not quite straight,' Mary observed; you were standing in front of her now. Had she reached forward to correct it you would have knocked her hand aside.

'Isn't it?' you responded, and turned to check in the mirror. The knot was a little high on one side.

You went through the movements of loosening it, then watched helplessly as all this sudden anger was squandered in positioning your tie more centrally. You pulled it so tight you almost choked yourself.

'That's much better,' said Mary, and kissed you.

'A quick drink before we go?' you suggested.

'Yes, that would be lovely. We've time for one,' she answered with a smile, meaning, of course, just one.

Then you trotted off to make it, this special treat before the big biscuit-night-out.

*

Almost four-thirty. The party was long over – and the morning-after just starting. The bedroom was becoming brighter: the walls, wardrobe, dressing table, chairs; everything was more visible now. Mary was still asleep. Carefully, without disturbing her, you got up, dressed, and went downstairs to the kitchen. You paused for a moment or two, as if unsure of why you were there, then, smiling to yourself, you opened the back door and stepped outside.

First light was colouring in the trees, the garden and the neighbouring houses – the entire world. Every second became a stronger affirmation of things. Their glory. First light was piercing you through with joy, hope. You walked out to the middle of the lawn, and there, raising your glass, which you must have picked up in the kitchen, toasted: 'Another day, another chance.'

The sun shone more brightly each moment. There was no mud. You could see clearly in all directions – and there was not a trace of mud. Not one smear.

And so, as the last stars disappeared before the mud began seeping in once more, you took your bearings from the early morning sunlight. Its clarity, its purity. Then you filled your glass again: a toast to everyone and everything on Earth – and everywhere beyond.

4

Elise was staring down at you. Outdoors. In the daylight. In the garden. The sky above her.

'Daddy?' she asked.

You were trying to keep your eyes open. You were lying on the lawn, your mouth too dry to speak. You were cold – the sun was shining. Brightly.

'Daddy?'

You sat up on one elbow, feeling sick momentarily.

Elise was still looking at you. If you stood up suddenly she would be frightened. It was difficult to hold on to her expression – you had to keep refocusing your eyes, concentrating hard. Every few seconds.

She began turning away.

'Elise . . .' you managed to say.

She stood still.

'Elise – Good morning,' you smiled.

Then, having refocused, you smiled again.

'Good morning,' you repeated, sitting up completely to bring yourself to her height.

She looked to one side as the brandy bottle rolled from your lap.

You both looked at it.

'It was empty anyway!' you remarked with a laugh.

She didn't reply.

'I got up early to see the dawn,' you went on to explain. 'It was a bit cold, and so . . .'

You gestured vaguely towards the bottle.

Finally she asked, 'Are you all right, Daddy?'

'Yes, of course.' Then, after a short pause, 'I'm fine. Fine.'

You smiled at her again.

She didn't move away, but looked in the direction of the house.

'Is Mummy up yet?' you asked a moment later.

She shook her head.

'And Tom?'

'No,' she answered almost reluctantly, as if you had been trying to force information from her.

'Let's keep it a secret then, eh?' you said, indicating the empty bottle.

She looked at the ground.

'A secret,' you repeated. 'Do you understand?'

You stood up a little unsteadily. Again a momentary sense of sickness.

The two of you walked back into the house, you carrying the brandy bottle and glass.

'Stay and play in the garden if you want,' you suggested. 'We'll have breakfast later on.'

Elise didn't reply at first; then she nodded: 'All right.'

'Would you like anything just now?' you asked her. 'Some cornflakes? Bread and honey?'

When she shook her head for the second time you began to feel anxious.

'A piece of chocolate?' Were you trying to bribe her?

She shook her head again.

'No thanks.'

'A secret, remember,' you stated again. 'Elise?'

'Yes, Daddy.' Then she turned and went back into the garden.

Quickly, you put the brandy bottle on the back shelf of the cupboard near the sink. That would do for the time being – the waste bin would have been too obvious. You wanted to get back upstairs and into bed before Mary woke up. It was still early.

You had just begun to climb the stairs when you met her coming down.

A moment's pause, then you said, 'Hello, I was just coming to wake you. It's a lovely day outside.'

She stopped a few steps above you. She had already dressed, but she could only just have got up. Did she believe you? It wasn't really a lie, anyway: it was a lovely day, and it would have been a good idea to have woken her, to have surprised her.

'Elise is already in the garden playing – and I thought it would be nice to have breakfast on the lawn,' you smiled. 'Fancy that?'

Mary didn't reply.

You repeated, 'It's a lovely morning.'

'When did you get up?' she asked abruptly.

'Oh, a while ago,' you replied. 'An hour or so, perhaps. It was so lovely that I couldn't stay in bed. I tried not to wake you,' you added.

As Mary didn't reply, you smiled again. The two of you stood quite still for a few seconds, you at the bottom of the stairs and she three or four steps above you.

'Well then,' you said eventually. *'Petit déjeuner sur l'herbe?* The kids will love it,' you added after a pause.

Mary had begun to come down the stairs – and before you could stop yourself you'd backed away from her, but recovered almost immediately. You took a step forward while reaching confidently for her hand to help her down from the bottom stair, as from a carriage.

'I hope you can do me the honour of breakfasting with me, ma'am?' you declared in a gentlemanly tone.

There was a moment's hesitation, then, smiling, she inclined her head graciously. 'You are too kind, sir.'

'A turn around the garden, perhaps, while it is being prepared? Everything there is in place. I have done what I could to arrange it to your comfort,' you continued as you led her through the kitchen. 'For the sky I have chosen a sea-blue with a few light clouds to relieve its—' You paused theatrically for a moment as though searching for the *mot juste*, 'its rather too-overwhelming grandeur. I trust this will suit.'

Mary was smiling.

'The weather is perfect, needless to say.'

'Of course.' She was almost laughing by this time.

'I have positioned a few stone walls to ensure we will not be disturbed, and some flowers, a lawn and a small tree. To promote a sense of place I have taken the liberty of suggesting a quiet suburban ambience – some houses in the background, birdsong, the sound of lawn-mowers and so forth. I hope it is to your satisfaction.'

You were standing at the back door now.

'And the breakfast itself?' enquired Mary, laughing.

'I was just getting round to that,' you replied with mock-peevishness. 'I've only been up an hour!' Then more briskly: 'I'll put the kettle on while you see the kids are all right.'

Mary went into the garden – and you relaxed.

As the breakfast preparations progressed, however, you went into decline – until by the time you heard the Shreddies rattling into the plates you were feeling very delicate indeed. Everything seemed metallic-grey, and you sensed that same colour inside you. So, before you served the family, you served yourself – and quickly. Brandy. And generously. Twice – skipping the toast (leave that until breakfast, you thought with a laugh) each time. The metal faded, and the kitchen and garden outside became coloured-in once more. Like drinking sunlight, almost.

After breakfast you felt well enough to go for the Sunday papers.

'Fancy coming with me?' you asked Elise.

'Okay, Daddy.'

It was a good ten minutes to the shop, and on the way back you began to go into decline again. You kept going. Elise was telling you about the different pets in her class at school: a hamster, a pussy, two rabbits—

Suddenly you became aware that everything around you was even greyer and more metallic-looking than before. You felt on fire – as if the sun had set somewhere inside you, its light straining to burn through your skin.

All at once you longed to tear yourself open – spilling colour upon the paving stones, the trees, the fence, the pillar-box – then fall back exhausted to let the light from deep inside you flood the sky with brightness.

You gripped your daughter's hand tightly. She was just coming to the end of her list of pets: '. . . and a hedgehog,' she concluded. 'Ouch, Daddy. That hurt!' She jerked her hand free.

'Sorry, Elise.' You met her glance rather uncertainly. 'I—'

'Don't you like animals?' she asked, taking your hand again.

'Some,' you replied. 'Lots of them really.'

You had to cross the road at this point – was that why she had taken your hand?

The two of you stood at the kerb while a van went past.

'What kinds most?' she asked as you began to cross.

'Oh,' you gestured vaguely. 'You know . . .'

Would she let go your hand when you reached the other side? You had not meant to hurt her. You continued: 'Different kinds . . . Some . . .'

Would she let go?

'Big ones?'

'Yes. Big ones.'

You had crossed the road and her hand was still in yours. A sense of relief.

It was a Sunday morning; you were walking down the street with your daughter, her hand in yours. You had just bought the Sunday papers and were taking them back to read with your wife. Everything was all right. Everything was fine.

'Big ones,' you repeated. 'Horses, giraffes, elephants, but most of all,' you paused, smiling, 'hippopotami.'

Elise looked up at you.

'Hippopotamuses you mean,' she corrected seriously.

'I know what I mean, young lady. Latinate plural: hippopotamus, hippopotami. And they wallow in the mud. You know the song?'

'What song?'

'The Mud Song, of course.'

You cleared your throat and began to sing loudly:

'Mud, mud, glorious mud,

Nothing quite like it for cooling the blood . . . '

By the end of the first verse you were singing very loudly, and were disappointed that Elise didn't join in. In fact she didn't say anything at all – even after you had finished. It had only taken you a short time to cover her pets, the rabbits, the cats and the hamsters, with your mud.

'See you later, Daddy,' she called out as you went in the front door and she turned round the side into the garden. You had let go her hand long before you came to the end of the song – the better to swing your arms in time to the music.

During a spartan lunch of no-gin-and-tonic, no-wine, with no-brandy to follow (at your suggestion, to reassure yourself that no-drink made no-difference) you sat, smiled, and made jokes. Lots of jokes. The accusations faced each other, and you faced your wife. The sun shone brightly. The flowers were growing. The grass was green.

The accusations were growing – and to prove it you had them measure each other every few minutes. They were laughing. Mary was smiling; you continued smiling and making jokes.

Afterwards you sat in a deckchair not-drinking, which was considered enough to keep you fully occupied. Every so often Mary glanced over to check that you were hard at work – which you were. Whenever you caught her doing this she smiled at you.

Mary, a great worker, keeps everything in the garden rosy. A few days after you'd moved into the house she began to lay a lawn lined with flowerbeds. Since then she's always managed, even in the middle of winter, to have a bit of colour somewhere. When one part of the garden fades, another is ready to take over – a kind of relay-race to Spring. Six Springs have been reached so far since moving here, albeit with a few fumbles during the hard frosts. Whatever the weather, she's out there gloved and galoshed if need be. Does she believe that if there is no green showing at any given moment then perhaps the race is lost and the entire garden ruined?

'Come on.' Mary had walked over to where you were sitting. 'How's about giving us a hand?'

You smiled and replied that you were very comfortable, thank you.

'Remember the Holy Book,' you cautioned. 'Six days shalt thou labour and do thy work, and on the seventh—'

'Don't worry yourself, all I want is to show you something. You just have to look and say how clever I am, green-fingered. That kind of thing.'

Not much to ask. You answered that you would be over in a few minutes.

'Oh, come on *now*,' she coaxed.

'What is it?'

'A surprise. Oh, come on!' she tried again.

She reached for you – and quite without thinking you pushed her hands roughly aside.

'In a few minutes,' you insisted.

Then, realising what you had done, you repeated more gently: 'I'll be over in a few minutes.'

You smiled and tried to take her hands.

She took a step backwards away from you.

'You bastard,' she said slowly.

'What's wrong with you?' you demanded. The tone of long-suffering in that unspoken 'now' inflected your question quite pitilessly, implying years of patient understanding on your part set against her persistent capriciousness. But you knew that she would accept it.

She was angry: 'I'm not asking much, am I? A few moments of your valuable idleness.'

Then, as you expected, she stopped.

'I'm sorry, Morris,' she began her apology.

'It's all right,' you replied with a weary magnanimity. You smiled effortlessly as usual, then continued: 'Let's see your surprise, then.'

You got out of your chair and, offering her your arm, began to make your way across the lawn to the right-hand corner of the garden where the accusations were digging in the flower-bed. Mary was saying something about how it was a good surprise, very unusual in fact, and that she had . . .

But you were having increasing difficulty in hearing her. It was as if, as soon as you had begun walking, someone had been gradually turning down the sound in the garden.

You continued walking.

'Mary!' you called out, and gripped her arm.

She looked at you. Panic must surely have been showing in your face. Everything seemed to be slowing down. It was an effort to place your feet one after another; you felt very heavy, as though the air pressure or gravity itself had been greatly increased.

She was telling you something; her lips were moving, but you could hear nothing of what she said. Her arm began to go round your waist, but how slowly everything was happening, how laboriously. It was becoming difficult to breathe; each breath was an effort, a greater and greater effort.

By the time you reached the accusations you were struggling for every breath. Slowly, very slowly they turned to face you. Tom's fringe took an unending length of time to settle. To be able to breathe you had to undo your tie and open the buttons of your shirt.

Mary's lips were moving again. You tried to make out what she was saying. She was pointing towards something in the flower-bed; all you were aware of, however, was your breathing as you forced your head down with an appalling slowness to look. Tom and Elise had moved to one side to let you see more clearly.

There was something in the earth, in the mud, something burrowing, trying to dig itself back into the ground away from the sunlight and the air.

Tom picked up a trowel and scooped busily at the mud to bring whatever it was back into view.

You felt you were about to collapse from lack of oxygen.

Each time the creature was almost exposed, the mud slid back on to it in slow motion. Elise began to help with the digging, then Mary. You no longer had the strength to gasp for another lungful of air – there was none anyway.

You turned and rushed back to the house – choking, bent almost double.

The cocktail cabinet was locked and the key missing. Where was it?

The door was glass-fronted. You could hardly breathe. Inside you could see a large bottle of gin. Your fingers slid across the glass panel; you were on your knees trying to prise open the door. Where was the key?

There were three bottles: gin, brandy and vodka. Standing behind the clear glass. And no key. You were choking, retching almost.

A moment later, the gin tasted like liquid oxygen. The pressure lifted immediately and you could breathe again. It was like surfacing; you took deep gulps of air.

Then you looked round to see Mary come in.

'Oh no, Morris! No!' she cried out.

But you were alert now – and backed away from her. She was not going to take the bottle away from you, not yet.

You took another drink. 'I was dying out there, dying – do you understand?'

Mary began to cry.

'I just needed one drink, that was all. I couldn't breathe.' You added: 'It's all right now.'

'One drink!' she exclaimed. 'Morris, you've drunk nearly half the bottle. And there's blood all over your—'

She started to cry again.

Half a bottle? No, not quite. But your hands and arms were covered in blood from smashing the glass front of the cocktail cabinet.

The two accusations had followed her in and were standing at the french windows.

'Mummy will be there in a minute.' Mary turned to them. 'Daddy's cut himself,' she added. 'We're just going to wash it and put on a band-aid.'

But Elise was already inside the room. She was standing a few feet away – staring at you. Was she too frightened to speak?

'I was thirsty, it was so hot – do you understand?' you explained to her.

She kept staring at you. Not a word. You wanted to have another drink – but not while she was watching, not against such silence. But if she turned to go away without saying a word . . .

'Elise,' you called after her.

'Elise!' you called louder, but she had already gone.

You remained staring at the place where she had been while Mary took the bottle from you. Then she led you into the kitchen to run your hand under the tap and wash off the blood. After she had done this she applied some TCP, all the time calling you a silly boy, a proper nuisance. She was brisk but very affectionate. Having examined the cut to check that it was clean, she bandaged it – not too loose, not too tight.

'That should do,' she said finally. You would have liked to kiss her at that moment, when she lifted up her head. But on the cheek. Were you too ashamed to kiss her on the lips?

'Thank you,' you managed to say in a clear voice, holding her gaze for as long as you could before having to look away. Was that genuine shame?

'Well,' she began, then put her hand on your arm so that you looked at her again. She smiled and continued: 'Well, we'd better pick up that broken glass – we don't want everyone cutting themselves, do we?'

She moved towards you and opened her arms. You embraced her, and for several seconds the two of you stood without speaking – your head on her shoulder.

Ten o'clock. The accusations were in bed, having looked in a medicinal half-bottle earlier to say goodnight to their dad who still felt a bit poorly after cutting himself so badly that afternoon. Tom asked if you'd lost lots of blood, and how much you would have needed to lose to kill you. Did you feel any lighter now? he wondered. Elise touched the back of your hand; you weren't sure if she did this accidentally or not as she reached over to kiss you. Then she said 'night-night' and immediately left the room.

Mary was downstairs watching TV.

Tomorrow was biscuit-Monday. You lay in bed watching the moon float slowly past the window, leaving in its wake a trail of weightless stars. You too were utterly weightless: you breathed deeply, the gills were still in good order after their day of rest. You had survived and returned to the ocean where you were born, washed there on a lulling tide of gin. Tomorrow would find you gently brought to shore.

Until then you could let yourself be carried by the current. A draught from the window made the partly-open curtains sway backwards and forwards to cast a reflection on the ceiling – like sunlight upon water. Lying on your back, you gazed straight ahead and could no longer tell whether you were above the surface looking down on the flowing water, or, as it seemed a moment later, were at a great depth looking up to where light broke against the far wall.

5

The alarm clock was ringing. It kept ringing.

You stopped it and lay there, wide awake. Helplessly and hopelessly wide awake. Monday morning. Mary was still asleep. Seven o'clock. Bright, bright outside.

Seven-o-two. Okay: up, up, and away. Up, up—

And dressed.

Downstairs and into the kitchen. Water on, toast on . . .

And into the bathroom. Splash on the face, splash in the pan . . .

And back. The toast gets turned, the pot gets filled, mind the snowman.

Off with the gas and out with the toast.

Snowman?

A snowman. In the middle of the kitchen. Standing perfectly still. He's looking at you. Smiling.

Smile back.

The snowman unfolds his arms and waves. Folds them again and smiles. You're dreaming. You must be.

But this is the kitchen, the teapot, the toast and the tea.

You're up and dressed and going to work. Majestic's.

But there he is.

He winks.

You need a drink. No.

Not that. Must be dreaming. Must be. Try a little test.

So you taste the toast and try the tea. You pinch yourself – all while the snowman watches.

And so – on with the radio full blast: the traffic news; seven-seventeen; the weather report, lovely summer's day.

The snowman scowls.

Change to Brahms – the snowman nods and taps his snowy feet in time.

One final test: you reach out to shake hands.

But the snowman won't.

Of course he won't! A short and melting introduction that would be!

Instead—

You take the kettle and pour boiling water onto the back of your hand.

And—

Nothing; nothing. Then pain; pain. Pain.

'Okay,' you say aloud. 'This is not a dream; I believe completely that this is not a dream.'

So either there is a snowman in the kitchen, or you need a drink.

The kitchen feels warm, doesn't it? And getting warmer.

You need a drink. You're shaking now. Look. A drink. A brandy. It's either that or snow-madness. And it's so warm in here.

A bottle, a glass – and here's to you, my abominable!

And nothing. Nothing, while the snowman watches.

He doesn't disappear. He watches. The brandy doesn't hit you. Not hard. Not at all. How hot it's getting.

Another brandy, and bigger. To you again.

Again nothing. The brandy doesn't hit and you have begun to sweat. The snowman looks, if anything, concerned.

Another, bigger brandy – and don't stop until the bottom.

'To you – a vanishing species,' you suggest.

This time, if anything, the snowman looks a little hurt.

The heat's become unbearable; the sweat's running into your eyes, your hands. You're wiping your brow; you've opened your shirt. You can hardly breathe – meanwhile the snowman looks on, cool, unmelted.

Angrier and angrier with every drink now – hotter.

The bottle's empty. You're roasting. You need that snowman. Badly. Near him the cold's delicious. You need to touch him. You want his icy forehead against yours – you need that snow-coolness.

You step towards him – closer. Another step. You reach out to touch him; you place your hand hard against him. You press your hand right into him. He begins to melt. You're wounding him. You stab him again and again. You grab handfuls of snow to rub on your burning face and chest. You're killing him.

Suddenly the doorbell rings. You stop for a moment – caught in the act.

The doorbell is ringing.

Then you laugh out loud, realising that no one need ever know: there'll be no evidence. You'll have nothing to hide! You'll tear at the snowman until he's melted into nothing. Let the doorbell ring, you'll answer it when—

The alarm was ringing. Monday morning. Mary switched it off and lay back in bed.

'God, do I feel tired!' she said. 'Mondays!'

It was a lovely summer's morning and you felt terrible. You didn't answer your wife, but kept still – you had enough to do simply lying there and feeling terrible.

'You'd better get up, Morris,' she prompted. 'It's almost five past, and—'

'I know, I know,' you interrupted, but not angrily. You weren't angry.

'Just reminding you.' Mary turned and kissed you.

Time to get up. You had to get up. Majestic Monday morning: new Monday clothes for a new week. Another biscuit week. You showered, shaved, got dressed.

'Shall I open the curtains?' You were standing at the window.

'Might as well,' answered Mary. 'It looks sunny outside.'

And she was right. The sun had already warmed the window-panes – even the wooden frame around the glass felt good to the touch. Outside, the part of the lawn nearest the house was brightly coloured, while the other remained in early morning shadow. The curtain being lifted for the opening scene, you thought to yourself: a summer's day, a biscuit day, a Majestic day!

'I'll put the kettle on,' you said, then went downstairs.

You entered the kitchen and switched on the radio, filling the room with a Vivaldi concerto—Opus 3, Number 8, for two violins. One of your favourites. It felt very warm, so, after putting on the water and lighting the gas, you opened the back door. The air was fresh and cool. You stood there for a few moments, breathing deeply.

You returned to the kitchen at the beginning of the slow movement in time to put on the toast.

You had poured in water to heat the pot and were coming back from emptying it when you remembered the snowman.

Of course! A snowman in the kitchen! You laughed to yourself and continued making the tea, putting in three teaspoonfuls: one for you, one for Mary and one for the pot.

That was all very strange, you thought to yourself: it was really hot, and then this snowman . . .

Suddenly, as you poured the water, you remembered the part about proving it wasn't a dream. All very strange. You had got up and come into the kitchen as usual, made tea and toast, then the snowman. You'd been making the tea and everything was as real as—

You stopped for a moment, putting down the kettle although you had not yet filled the pot, and remarked half aloud: 'As real as this.' You paused briefly, then glanced around – but of course there was nothing. No snowman. Just the kitchen: the pots, pans, cooker, the table, the chairs, the posters on the wall. Everything as it should be.

You continued making the tea, pouring the rest of the water into the pot – and then you remembered that in the dream, also, everything had been exactly as it should be. Except for the snowman.

You placed the lid on the teapot and were beginning to feel a little anxious. Of course, you could always prove that it wasn't a dream, couldn't you? By pouring boiling water on the back of your hand, for example.

There was no need to slam the teapot down on the sideboard. No need to get anxious, it would only make things worse. Your hand was shaking. You didn't want Mary to see that, not after the previous day's little disaster with the cocktail cabinet.

'Daddy, the toast's burning!' Elise was standing at the cooker watching large flames that had begun coming from the grill-pan underneath.

Into the sink with it: toast, grill-pan and all. Start again.

'Go and get washed, Elise.' You needed room – Mary and Tom would be down at any moment.

'But I've already washed, Daddy. I'm all ready for breakfast now,' she declared proudly.

'Well, sit down then.' But you didn't mean to be angry. You repeated more gently: 'Sit down, please, Elise,' and you smiled at her.

Having dried the grill-pan, you took fresh bread and tried again. You brought tea, milk, sugar, butter, marmalade; plates, cups, saucers, knives, spoons over to the table and told Elise to sit up straight. The snowman had gone. If you managed to get breakfast right, everything else would follow.

'Daddy, the toast's burning again.' Elise was laughing.

Mary had come into the kitchen. Your hands were shaking. The grill-pan rattled against the cooker as you lifted it out. You could feel sweat breaking out on your brow.

'Morris?' Mary was standing behind you – ready to be understanding. You would have to turn to look at her.

'Morris?' She placed her hand on your shoulder; in a

moment she would come round to stand beside you. Her hand was warm – and briefly you wished that you were a snowman so that her touch would melt into you, soothing the pain deep inside. The pain that you yourself are unable to reach.

'I'm all right, Mary,' you turned, and said with a smile: 'Let's have breakfast.'

Tom and Elise were there too, looking at you.

'Division of labour,' you announced. 'Tom, put these in the bin,' indicating the burnt toast. 'Elise, more bread.'

The accusations did this.

'Monday mornings, eh?' you smiled at Mary.

'Maybe if you—?' she began.

'I'm fine,' you interrupted firmly in answer to whatever she was going to suggest.

'How's the toast doing, kids?' you asked.

In less than two hours you would be at your office.

6

Katherine hadn't yet been in with the Majestic mail and the diary, so there was still time for a quick glance round your office, round your third-floor mud-trap. Time for a last-minute check to see that everything was in place: the files in their correct order, the pens primed, the pencils sharpened, the calendar at the correct date.

Across the car park at the loading bay opposite, the men had been working since eight that morning, bringing large boxes on trolleys to fill the lorries. They had begun when you were still eating breakfast, and they'd still be hard at it long after you'd left for home. You earn over five times what they do, plus perks. No one would give you a row or cut your pay for being an hour late, or for choosing to leave an hour early. It makes you feel bad to think of them – yet that morning, like every morning, you devoted a few moments to standing at the window and feeling bad. You realise, of course, that in the same time someone somewhere has probably made a phone call and earned himself ten times your salary – but you are never sure whether that thought makes you feel better or worse.

You turned from the window to give the room a final once-over.

Everything was exactly as it should be: the blue door, the light-blue carpet, the executive swivel for you, the padded straight-backs for visitors, the desk-light, the telephone, the multicoloured graphs on one wall, the matching

Mondrian on the wall opposite. You crossed the floor to make sure your coat was hanging securely on its peg – you didn't want it falling down suddenly during an important meeting.

But it was fine. Everything was fine. Monday morning. A Majestic Monday morning – and you were ready. Quite ready.

Katherine would be in at any moment. You were ready for her. Ready and waiting.

She would bring mail needing to be answered, and the diary setting out the rest of the day in intervals of thirty minutes. There would be plenty to do. Plenty to keep you busy.

The phone rang: 'Call from Mr Lowestoft, Mr Magellan, on line two.'

Lowestoft – and it was only just nine-thirty!

'Thank you, Katherine.' You pressed for line two.

Pencil and paper at the ready. You almost laughed aloud, but managed not to.

'Good morning, Dan,' you greeted him.

'Morning, Morris.'

You drew a line across the page: words above, illustrations below, as per usual.

'A good weekend?' you asked, knowing quite well he would want to get straight to the biscuit-talk.

'Yes, thank you, Morris. Yourself?'

You smiled to yourself at this little victory won for the real world. A small vertical line in the centre of the illustration section. The side of a house? The trunk of a tree?

'Very pleasant, but quiet you understand. We needed a chance to get the feet up after that "Best of British" knees-up, you might say,' you replied with a laugh.

You were ready for some party gossip about one of the publicity-biscuits when—

'Sorry to start ripples so early in the day,' interrupted Lowestoft.

Another vertical line, then a few horizontals – rippley ones of course.

'But I think we should get together before the wrapper conference this afternoon,' he continued.

'Something up?' you asked, shifting to anxiety-tone.

To the two verticals you added a horizontal base, joining them and extending a little on either side. A biscuit-box being loaded on to the top of a lorry to suggest a touch of social view-out-of-the-window realism? Or maybe a topless top hat?

'Well, Morris. I've got a short report in front of me from Bowen.'

'Yes?' Interest-tone.

'According to him, Bateman's department have got it all wrong as far as orange is concerned. Also,' he continued, 'he says that the typeface is too "squeamish", whatever that means.'

He paused for you, for the affirmative half-laugh. Dutifully you filled the gap, then dropped a couple of diagonals from the horizontal. It was coming clear now: a ship, a small yacht perhaps.

Lowestoft continued: 'And is quite out of the question. "Out of the question" underlined.'

Right enough – and you joined the two diagonals to give the base of the ship.

'Underlined *twice*. Are you with me, Morris?'

Not twice, not really – unless you made it into a catamaran. Instead you added a couple of seagull ticks before beginning on the sails.

'Yes,' you responded firmly. Deliberation-tone. 'Sounds like big trouble.'

'You said it, Morris. Big trouble.'

He paused again. You half-laughed for him once more, and added a small pennant to each mast. It was coming along rather nicely – a two-masted schooner, ocean-going. You sketched in the sun, and the shadow of the ship wavering artistically under the hull.

A lorry started up outside.

'So we'd better have a chat and get ourselves sorted out,' urged Lowestoft.

'I agree,' you responded with conviction, while outlining an island, or a small whale perhaps, in the left-hand corner.

'Lunch?'

You settled for a whale, and converted the start of a palm-tree into a water-spout.

'Fine,' you answered. 'In the exec?'

'Twelve-thirty suit?'

'Should do; I'll check with Katherine and if need be get back to you; but it's all right as far as I remember.'

You wanted to put yourself somewhere in the picture now – on board if possible. But the sails were rather large. A problem.

'Right you are then, Morris. Goodbye.'

'Bye.' You put down the phone.

Maybe you could have just gone for a swim. But the whale? They're plankton-eaters, you thought, but weren't sure. Better to be on the safe side, so you drew yourself close to the side of the ship. You picked up the phone and replaced it again so the wire wasn't tangling all over the desk.

'Wrappers,' you thought aloud.

Something that Turner, the former Head of Sales, had once said occurred to you: 'We are selling biscuits, and we must never lose sight of that fact. Biscuits.' Everyone at the meeting had nodded. You had nodded too; in fact you had been rather moved by his simple declaration.

Were you close enough to the boat? You wished you could rub out the small figure and position it even nearer. Perhaps if it became another whale, a smaller, strictly vegetarian one, then you could—

A knock on the door, and Katherine entered.

'Good morning, Mr Magellan.'

'Good morning, Katherine.'

You smiled at each other, then she took her seat beside your desk. A light blue summer's dress; a silver bracelet and chain; the slightest eye-shadow.

'A good weekend?' you asked her.

'So-so,' she shrugged. 'You know how it is.' She put down the mail and diary next to your boat, then continued: 'Only I'm so tired on Monday mornings I sometimes wonder if it's worth it – and broke!' she added, laughing.

Very deliberately you kept your attention on her and didn't glance once at the letters, but edged them along casually with your hand to cover your seascape. It's good to be able to chat with her like this – for although she is your secretary, professionally speaking, nevertheless you get on well with each other. She knows she can confide in you, if she needs to.

She told you about her weekend: a girlfriend round for dinner on Friday; shopping on Saturday – after rather a late start, she admitted with a laugh; the pub and then dancing on Saturday night. She has been your secretary for just over a year now; a very bright girl.

Definitely a unique friendship. It's hardly the same with the others, those in the typing pool. When you go there they stop chatting and laughing among themselves. They talk to you of course – but it feels different, unequal. Like a teacher with his pupils, except that they're always on their best behaviour. You do the best you can to make things easier for them, more relaxed. Although you are their boss you try to have a chat and a laugh with them whenever possible.

'And I suppose you'll be burning it up at the weekend, Barbara?' you had asked one of them on the Friday before the 'Best of British' do. You didn't know where the phrase 'burning it up' had come from, but it sounded appropriate. The girl, a redhead who was sitting two machines along from where you stood, looked up and smiled slightly.

You tried again. A *double-entendre* to ease the teacher-pupil politeness. 'I mean, Barbara,' you hesitated briefly, 'I'm sure you'll be burning it at both ends!'

The girl glanced around nervously; she'd stopped smiling. You were about to repeat the question with a jocular 'You there! Girl in the third row,' the memory of which would bring out a cold sweat on you now – when she spoke: 'A bit, I suppose, but . . . ' then she added uncertainly: 'But my name's not Barbara.'

You could almost hear the unspoken 'sir', before she added as though to help you, 'That's Barbara over there,' and she pointed to a girl in the next aisle who also had red hair.

'I'm Mary,' she explained. Embarrassed.

There was silence for a moment. You salvaged the situation for her as best you could by remarking that your wife was also called Mary. Quite a coincidence. But her only response was a pupil-polite: 'Really?'

Right from the very start, however, it has been different with Katherine. Paternal almost.

'And you, Mr Magellan?' she asked. 'Did you have a good weekend?'

'Fine, thank you, Katherine,' you smiled. 'Probably a little less exhausting than yours,' you laughed. 'Rather quiet, in fact. The "Best of British" do on Saturday night pretty much took care of Sunday!' You laughed again, and she laughed.

'You didn't miss much there, Katherine, I can tell you. The same old faces and the same old wives. Then Sunday in the garden just taking our time and pleasing ourselves.'

You paused for a moment, remembering how pleasant it had been having a family breakfast on the lawn before strolling with Elise for the papers, then some light gardening.

'Yes,' you continued, 'it's a rule I make for myself: the office is the office and home is home.' You smiled at her. She smiled back.

'Yes,' you relaxed back in the executive swivel. 'Six days shalt thou labour and then rest upon the seventh. Remember? Only it's usually the sixth and seventh day now. That's progress!' You laughed again. Katherine smiled.

'No,' you resumed after a short pause. 'Come the weekend I leave the work behind; shut up shop Friday at four, and sometimes a little earlier!' you laughed. Then continued a moment later: 'And shut up shop, as I said. Then home, and forget about it until Monday.'

Katherine continued looking at you. She had said nothing.

'Which is today, I'm afraid. So let's see what it has brought us.' You indicated the papers on the desk.

She picked up the letters and began to summarise them, then went through the diary of the day's appointments. To do this more clearly she got up and stood quite close to your desk, at the side.

'You could mark down, just to keep the record straight, that I'm lunching with Mr Lowestoft at twelve-thirty.'

'Yes, Mr Magellan.'

Sometimes, as she handed you a letter, your fingertips touched, but you continued talking quite naturally.

'Thank you, Katherine,' you'd say as you studied its contents.

You decided that once she'd gone you would give the entire wrapper scenario a quick once-over. You'd ask her to bring the necessary files just before she left.

There was brandy in the desk. Not that you needed any, of course, but still, it was good to know that it was there. At least you're sociable. It's only politeness. Colleagues know that if there's to be a meeting in your office you'll do the courtesy of offering them a drink. Brandy usually, but you have some whisky and sherry. Gin is too fiddly, what with the lemon, tonic, ice-cubes and so on. You're not a cocktail bar, after all.

Brandy's the best – and simplest. Courvoisier. A name to be spoken slowly, to be enunciated, letting the syllables slide languorously around inside your mouth. Courvoisier, you repeated into yourself like an incantation, a blessing.

Sunday: not only had you lost the key to the drinks cupboard, you remembered suddenly, but you had to force the lock, and cut yourself – all for a post-prandial *digestif*, as the French so charmingly call it, for yourself and Mary. You needed a stiff drink after that, a medicinal one. The glass had cut deep. You still felt a bit dicky, in fact. A kind of delayed shock – you nearly fainted at the time, but not quite. You would shortly have to deal with the wrapper report for that afternoon – and weren't really yet back to AI. You still didn't feel a hundred per cent. A quick tonic to clear the brain. No point trying to do the job half-arsed and half-asleep. And so, once Katherine had gone . . .

The thing about drink is knowing how to use it – and

not letting it use you. One drink'll charge the system, get it in gear; but a second could be too much. Knowing when to drink and when to stop – that's the trick.

'Some wine with lunch?'

'Not for me, Morris, thank you,' said Lowestoft.

'A beer then?' you suggested.

'No.'

He'd hesitated. You looked at him and smiled. And kept smiling.

'Okay,' he relented. 'Make it a lager.' You relaxed and considered the menu. Executives eat well – and not a biscuit in sight. After some careful reflection you ordered duck, with chocolate mousse to follow. When the drinks arrived Lowestoft said: 'Cheers!'

'And here's to wrapping up the wrapper conference this afternoon,' you added.

The beer tasted thin after the brandy.

'Now,' you began, having put down your glass, 'what's all this about the orange wrapper and the "squeamish" typeface?'

Yes, maybe you do have a drink now and again, but no one could ever say it affected your work. No chance. You're good. Bloody good. One of the youngest executives in the business. On the ball. Always.

Lowestoft was still talking, and you noticed your glass was almost empty. The food had not arrived and you were getting hungry.

'God, they're taking their time, aren't they?' you observed.

He nodded, and was about to continue his wrapper story when you pointed to his glass and gestured to ask if he wanted another. He shook his head.

The wrapper story proceeded one word at a time. You glanced over at the waitress, indicating your empty glass. Then turned back to Lowestoft and his wrapper-words.

When your drink arrived you took a sip, then put down your glass, and, neatly interrupting Lowestoft, made the comment: 'So, it's the Heinz Baked Bean story all over again. Change the wrapper from orange to blue, and Bowen reckons sales will be up thirty per cent. Is that it?'

Not a bad summary of Lowestoft's rambling analysis. On the ball as ever.

'More or less,' he answered. 'According to Bowen, it's . . . '

Bowen. The Gospel according to Bowen. A sideways promotion if there ever was one. And there he was, still trying to get himself in with his 'squeamish typeface' and 'negative customer response to the colour orange'. Some chance.

'At last!' you remarked when eventually the food did arrive. 'That's one way to sell beer, anyway – starve them into submission!'

Lowestoft didn't reply, and you ordered another drink.

Majestic meetings are a very dry business – in every sense of the word. One, two, and sometimes even three, very parched hours. Dry as a biscuit. A room full of Batemans and Bowens hard at the biscuit-banter. You, however, have perfected the old 'papers back at the office' routine. A classic. A winner every time. Two minutes: the missing pages beside the brandy and glass, filed and ready in the top drawer. A life-saver. A half-time oasis-halt. Then it's back to the desert wastes: the shifting graphs, the trends and counter-trends, the biro-clicks and calculator-bleeps.

After the meeting Lowestoft walked back with you along the corridor, saying he didn't know how you did it. A few beers at lunchtime and he would have been flat out. 'But you,' he declared, 'pulled us all through. Quite brilliant.' His very words. Brilliant.

Into your office at last. You sat down and swivelled briefly, then stood up and looked out of the window. The vast biscuit tins as usual: the loaders were still loading, the lorries were still leaving, and the sky remained a clear, immaculate and oceanic blue.

Lowestoft was right: that was a great meeting. No doubt about it. And it was all at your fingertips: facts, figures, and examples. Bowen's report and Bateman's proposals dealt with in a couple of sentences. Death sentences. Then those theories about colour and emotion, from Goethe to NASA reports, that you suddenly remembered from goodness knows where. The confidence, the style, the jokes, the seriousness – playing one executive-biscuit against another, then arbitrating at exactly the right moment and in exactly the right tone of voice. Like a conductor who knows in advance the sound he wants from his players, you knew exactly what you wanted – and got it!

You surely deserved a drink after that – and no mistake!

Courvoisier. Then you poured one for Courvoisier, for Monsieur Courvoisier himself. He deserved it. You got them through, and he got you through – not really, of course, but you needed that little something extra, that oasis-halt. A little inspiration.

Anyway, you took a drink and let the drink take a drink. Then one for the train, then home.

7

And so – it was goodbye to Katherine and out through the open-plan, down the lift, past the potted plants, the low tables. The plate-glass doors, the drive, the Majestic Main Gate. Then along the narrow lane to the station.

You waited on the platform with your ticket and the evening paper.

The train arrived. You got in, sat down, and began reading.

'Doesn't have a future?' the man opposite exclaimed in mock surprise. 'He doesn't have a past either, not now. He's a drunk.'

You glanced up. Two men were sitting opposite you, two men you had never seen before. They must have been talking about someone else. They must have been. Not you. They didn't know you. You didn't look drunk. You weren't drunk – you were reading the evening paper. One of them noticed you were watching them – and so, back to your paper. You were reading. You couldn't be drunk. Not if you were reading.

'Doesn't have a future, doesn't have a past either – he's a drunk,' the man had said. No future, no past – that left only the present, you thought to yourself. But there are two kinds of present, aren't there: the one with a drink, and the one without. Hardly a difficult choice. For you.

Also, you thought, there are only two places in the world: where there is a drink, and where there isn't.

Somewhere – and nowhere. But you know where you are with it. You know it will get you through. You know when to stop. No slurring and falling over for you. You know exactly what you're doing: enough, or too much. That's your rule – and you know exactly when enough is about to become too much. You're aware of what's happening. Your work's going well. What a meeting you'd just had; 'Brilliant,' said Lowestoft, his very words. 'Brilliant.' Your family has its ups and downs, of course – but what family doesn't? No, you were no drunk. Couldn't be.

Not like Sammy, the old dead-beat who had lived in the flat opposite when you were a student. Now, there was a drunk. You'd come home at night to find him on the stairs – back from a day at the business college to that bundle of clothes and sick blocking up the entrance. You helped him the first few times – stood him on his feet, kept him on his feet, then hauled him, a step at a time, all the way up to his front door. Real life, you thought.

No, you're no drunk. You work – and work well. Brilliantly, according to some. You're looked up to. Respected.

That was when you decided: the next time Katherine gave you some letters, you would let your fingers touch hers as they had last time, and then – just the slightest pressure. See what happened. She wasn't a child. Nothing too obvious, of course. The slightest pressure, a glance. She's a really good girl – understands you much better than Mary, much better. She listens to you, then has something interesting to say herself. She dresses well.

Just a glance – she'd get the message. She'd smile and put down her notepad, then come round to your side of the desk. There would be no need to say anything – she'd understand completely. Yes. Katherine. It wasn't just sex, of course. That was no problem – you could have any of the typists you wanted. You're the boss. They like you. Who else chats and banters with them? Gets on so well? No, it's not sex, but affection. Real affection. That's what you feel for her – and it's returned. No doubt about that. No doubt at all, you decided.

When you'd shown her the photographs of the Portugal holiday she had leant close to you, her hair almost touching the side of your cheek. She placed her hand very close to yours and pointed to one of the statues.

'What's that, Mr Magellan?' she asked. Very interested.

'A statue of one of the family,' you replied with a laugh.

'What family?'

'Mine – who else?'

'Yours?'

'Naturally. Ferdinand Magellan, explorer extraordinaire! First man round the world and back again.'

Katherine looked at you. She seemed puzzled for a moment, then she smiled. A delightful, hesitant smile.

A few moments later she asked: 'And that's your wife, is it?'

You nodded.

'A nice hat she's wearing,' she commented. Then she glanced at you.

You didn't reply immediately but looked at her, into her eyes. That moment's pause was your real response. She understood that your remarks about the weather, the beach, the food et cetera were just words. Everything was expressed in your silence. Katherine looked away, slightly embarrassed, but pleased. You almost kissed her then.

Yes, you decided: a glance, a discreet touch, would be enough.

The two men sitting opposite got to their feet and went to the door. The train was slowing down. Drunks – what did they know about it? You could see them under the table any day of the week. Bowen/Batemans the lot of them. Under the table with them, and you'd still take the biscuit at any wrapper rap. Drunk – they didn't know the meaning of the word.

When the train reached your station you got off and began to walk quickly home. There was nothing like a good day at the office to set you up for dinner.

'He's a fool,' you were telling Mary.

It was nearly eight o'clock: the roast was in the oven, the veg in the pot. The table was neatly laid: knives, forks, spoons – all shining; clean plates, glasses and serviettes. Mary was in her armchair, understanding as ever. You were in your armchair, working hard at the g-and-t and spattering mud over everything. The accusations were safely in bed.

'Bowen's a fool,' you repeated, 'a complete fool. He tries, I suppose, but he's a sideways promotion – and knows it! Never stops. He's heading for a crack-up.'

You were telling her about the meeting, about you, about them, about who's cracking up. You could feel the mud filling your mouth – and the more you spat out, the more there seemed to be. It was rising in you like sickness.

If only Mary would interrupt you. If only she would say, 'Morris, calm down,' or, 'I'm sure it's not really as bad as that.'

After six years of marriage you needed to alter, only slightly, the tone of your voice to lacerate her.

'Do you agree?' you taunted.

She did not reply.

You decided to wait for as long as you could before attacking her silence – like holding back when making love.

'The pork must be nearly ready,' Mary stated suddenly, and stood up.

Everything that evening – the glass you were drinking from, the plates, even the knives and forks – seemed brittle. The dining room seemed certain to crack from side to side if you replaced your wine glass awkwardly. You drank to put yourself beyond this fragility, to reach *terra firma*.

When you were a child you had a radio with a 'magic eye' – a green light that shone brightest when the signal was at its strongest; a little off the station and its brightness faded, as though with disappointment. That evening, with each glass of wine, you sensed your 'magic eye' shining brighter and brighter. Until finally the continuous interference, the mud that was all around and inside you, completely disappeared – and you could see everything exactly as it was. Then you could spy with your magic eye something beginning with—

Mary looked at you, puzzled. You must have spoken aloud.

'It was green,' you explained.

'Pardon?'

'Green. The magic eye in our radio.'

'What magic eye? What are you talking about, Morris?' she asked.

You wanted to describe how it had shone so extraordinarily bright whenever—

'Extraordinarily.' In silence you enunciated these syllables into yourself without once faltering. But to speak them aloud – ah, your mud-mouth!

You were standing by the sideboard; Mary was a few feet away. Elise and Tom were by the doorway. They looked half-asleep. Mary was wearing her dressing gown.

'It's all right, darlings,' she said to the accusations, who were keeping very close together.

'It's all right,' she repeated. 'Daddy and I couldn't sleep, that's all. We're sorry if we woke you. Let's all go back to bed.'

They went towards her, and she looked at you over Tom's head. Before you could say anything, however, Elise asked: 'Why have you got a piece of wood, Daddy?'

You didn't understand.

'That piece of wood in your hand,' she insisted.

You looked down. In your right hand there was a piece of wood like a club. You were gripping it tightly.

'I—' you began, but stopped almost immediately and looked down at it again.

'Because,' Mary interrupted to cover your hesitation, 'because we thought we heard a mouse. And you know how scared Mummy is of mice.'

Elise giggled – then looked worried. 'Was there one?'

Mary managed to smile. 'No, dear. Or, if there was, it's gone.'

Was that what you had been doing? Chasing mice? You were wearing your pyjamas and were in your bare feet.

'Maybe it was – a burglar!' Tom suggested in a sudden and frightening voice to his sister. Elise looked alarmed. Then he added quickly: 'Or a ghost!' and he raised his arms, 'Whoo!'

'Be quiet, Tom, and don't be silly,' Mary said sharply. 'Whatever it was, it's gone now – hasn't it?' she asked you.

The three of them turned to you; you put down the wood on the top of the sideboard.

'It's gone,' you agreed, 'and it's time everyone else was gone too – to bed! Come along. Chop-chop!'

Having put the accusations to bed, the two of you returned to your room. Mary didn't speak, and once you were both in bed she switched off the light. You lay for several minutes without saying anything. It must have been the middle of the night. Only then did you realise how cold you were. You reached for Mary's hand and held it. After a moment you squeezed it, but there was no response. You could tell from her breathing, however, that she was not asleep.

You longed to put your arm around her. Her hand felt quite lifeless in yours – but warm. You wanted to speak. You squeezed her hand again – and waited. Still there was no response. It occurred to you that this was rather like ringing a doorbell, but there was no one in. You almost laughed aloud. Should you try ringing again?

'Go to sleep, Morris,' said Mary abruptly in a clear voice.

'Mary, I—'

'Go to sleep. We'll talk about it in the morning.'

'About what? Mary, I want to understand what—'

'*You* want to understand?' she repeated scornfully.

Then she added something, but too quietly for you to catch it.

'Sorry?' you said after a pause, 'I didn't quite . . . '

'I said "Jesus Christ!", Morris,' she answered angrily. 'Now go to sleep – and let me sleep.' Her voice was very firm.

'Are you angry?' you asked after a few seconds – and immediately wished you hadn't.

'For Christ's sake, Morris!' Mary sat up in bed and snapped on the light. 'Are you so drunk that—? Of course I'm angry!' She glared at you.

She was between you and the bed-light, and when she moved slightly the light shone directly into your eyes. It was very bright; you put your hand up to shield them. Mary backed away from you suddenly.

'I'm not going to—' You were shocked.

'I don't know what you're going to do,' she cried out, 'and I don't think you do either.'

For several seconds the two of you sat staring at each other. She was angry and you felt bewildered. You couldn't understand what was wrong – something had happened, but you had no idea what. However, to show that there were no hard feelings, and to demonstrate that you really did care, you placed your hand gently on her arm.

She shook it off.

'Don't you touch me,' she said fiercely. Then after a moment she added more calmly: 'Let's leave this till tomorrow. I'm very tired, Morris, very tired.'

She didn't smile; instead she reached to switch off the light. Before she did, you said, 'Goodnight.' She did not reply.

The two of you were lying a few inches apart, in silence. That she had not said goodnight, you felt, somehow put you in the right. Your eyes were wide open and you were completely wide awake. It required an effort to resist the temptation to take her hand again. You wanted to. You knew it would make her angry – yet you still wanted to. You could anticipate her response, her snatching it away and shouting at you while you pleaded affection – which, of course, would only make things worse. You knew exactly what would happen.

Before you could stop yourself you had said her name aloud: 'Mary.'

Without a word your wife got up. You watched as she put on her dressing gown and bent down for her slippers. Her silhouette moving in the darkened room, angrily.

Without speaking. There was nothing you could say, not now. You heard the door close behind her.

She had gone to sleep in the spare room. Even then you wanted to follow her, to apologise, to plead forgiveness, to make promises. Briefly you pictured yourself lying in her arms, reconciled, the two of you embracing each other lovingly – but then almost immediately you returned again to the moment of pleading, of begging.

Having lain back down on the bed, you began going over everything that had just occurred, repeating each phrase again and again. Repeating her anger. Repeating those gestures of compromise you knew would push her to more anger.

8

The alarm clock kept ringing. Mary wasn't there. You felt sick. Bright sunlight kept coming into the room. She was in the spare room. You were going to be sick. Downstairs, holding a piece of wood. Mary had gone to sleep in the spare room. If you got up immediately maybe you wouldn't be sick. Your head hurt, and your stomach—

Your head really hurt. A medicinal hair of the dog. The accusations had been in the front room as well. The middle of the night. And her anger. Her anger. A hair of the dog. In its kennel behind the wardrobe. But you weren't up to whistling for it, not yet. Soon. The vertical was hard enough – keep the head down and you'd survive.

Almost there. Good dog. Nice dog. Didn't need to sit or beg, not for you. Didn't need to wag its tail either. You'd do that yourself. 'Cheers' to the dog. To man's best friend. Then 'Cheers' to yourself.

Patting the dog once more to be on the safe side. Shower, then on with the biscuit-suit and downstairs to the kitchen.

An empty kitchen. You decided to skip the Shreddies and Mozart that morning. No time. Work. Work. Biscuits.

A quick note to the family: Have a good day, love and kisses – to show them everything was all right. Which it was. Another kiss to make sure, the clincher – you almost laughed aloud but managed not to. And out the door.

An early walk, lovely morning. Luckily you brought the

dog with you. A breath of fresh air. Patting the dog when no one was about. The station. Six stops. Another dog-hair before you arrived at number six. He was nearly bald by now, and so a slight detour was necessary – to call in at a friendly neighbourhood pet shop.

Then the Majestic Main Gate, the drive, the plate-glass doors, the lift, the open-plan, the office, and a working breakfast for you and your four-legged friend. Another day, another slide through the mud.

Katherine, letters, a report, going out every so often to the executive cloakroom to give the dog another pat – but privately. No pets allowed.

Lunch, and back to the afternoon mud-trap.

Katherine's intercom voice:

'Mr Lowestoft and Mr Bowen are here, sir.'

'Very good, Katherine,' you replied. 'Show them in.'

A social call? Should you remain seated behind the desk, or rise to the occasion? You hesitated. Before you could come to a final decision, however, your visitors had entered, greeted you, and sat down.

'Dan. Larry.' You smiled, nodding to each of them in turn. You stood up, then sat down again. A moment's pause. Katherine came in and took her usual seat, with a writing pad on her knee. A formal meeting, it appeared. An anti-social call. Lowestoft was looking at you. Bowen was glancing round the room. Katherine was waiting for the meeting to begin. You also were waiting for the meeting to begin, waiting for them to explain why they'd come. More about the wrapper, perhaps?

You were about to invite them to start when Lowestoft cleared his throat – and said nothing. Katherine looked up. Had she stenographed the cough? you wondered, almost laughing aloud, and the hesitant quality of the silence perhaps?

'You were wanting to clarify a few points, you said,' Bowen announced suddenly.

You were? Then before you could reply, he continued: 'Not that there can be much to add after yesterday. Unless you just want to rub it in. Ignore that, please,' he added, turning to Katherine. He didn't smile.

Had *you* called the meeting? Were Bowen and Lowestoft there because you had asked them? And Katherine, to make the whole thing official? They were waiting for you. Let them. A glance at the Mondrian, then at the multicoloured graphs, at the well-ordered files running Jan–Mar; April–June; July–Sept. Blue files like the blue door. You picked up a pen and glanced at your visitors. Then at Katherine.

'Are you ready?' you asked her.

'Yes, sir,' came the reply.

'Very good then,' you nodded to her and shuffled a few papers that were to hand on your desk. You put down the pen and using both hands stacked the papers more neatly. Another glance at Lowestoft and Bowen. Then at the papers: expenditure chits.

'Now,' you addressed the two men.

The noise of a lorry starting up outside. You glanced towards the window. It was a beautiful summer's day. Hot. All at once it felt stifling in your office. A lorry was being loaded at the bay opposite. You imagined the men in their shirt-sleeves pushing trolleys stacked high with large boxes.

Eight boxes is the most that can be carried in one trip. You remembered this from having spent a week in dispatch when you first joined Majestic's. Quite a skill too – you had tried balancing the top one with your free hand, took three steps, and immediately dropped the lot. The men laughed at the junior executive, not at all unkindly, and helped you try again. You needed two helpers to reach the lorry. 'Tacking because of high winds,' you explained as you zig-zagged unsteadily across the loading bay with your extra crew. Everyone was laughing, you especially. You felt happy. The driver was called Bev – and while you were resting afterwards you watched him do handstands in the back of his half-empty lorry. He would hook his feet under one of the side supports, then lift himself up from the ground.

'Before we begin, I'll open the window slightly if nobody minds. It's very hot in here,' you announced.

Lowestoft and Bowen looked at each other but made no comment. Katherine said nothing. You stood up and unclasped the snib to slide the window open. You could hear the men's voices; there was a smell of baking and a draught of warm air. Another lorry started up, revving noisily. Too noisily. You reclosed the window immediately, then turned back to face into the room.

The three of them – Lowestoft, Bowen and Katherine – were looking at you. Lowestoft, however, was now standing right beside you. Involuntarily you stepped back against the radiator. When had he stood up? Bowen was smoking a cigarette.

'Are you feeling all right, Morris?' Lowestoft asked.

'Fine,' you replied. Then repeated: 'Fine. I just wanted a bit of fresh air – but there was too much CO out there!' You laughed.

'But—' Bowen was about to speak when Lowestoft glanced at him and he stopped. You, however, noticed that at once. You were on the ball. As always.

'Maybe you'd better sit down now, and we can begin,' suggested Lowestoft.

'Maybe we'd *all* better sit down now, and I can begin,' you declared with emphasis. Back in control. You would show them now. These biscuit-men. Show them? You would eat them! You almost laughed aloud.

'Okay, Katherine?' you enquired.

'Yes, sir, I'm ready,' she replied.

You were glad she was there: now she could see you in action.

You paused briefly, then began.

'Colours . . . ' you paused again for effect, then continued: 'Colours – are they more important than biscuits? We have many elements involved here: the primary and secondary qualities of biscuits, as Locke might have called them. Locke with an "e" at the end,' you added with a smile, turning to Katherine. 'Colour, design, typeface, price, shape, weight and so on are all secondary qualities. The one that's primary, the only one that's primary in this Lockean sense, is the biscuit itself. Now . . . ' you continued, seeing that Bowen was about to interrupt with one of his sideways promotion ideas. 'Now, only the consumer who has already tasted the biscuit knows the taste, that is, knows the *real* biscuit. It follows therefore that the secondary qualities alone must determine his initial choice.

'What are we to make of this? That . . .' Again you had to talk through another Bowen interruption.

'That,' you repeated firmly, 'our first priority must be appearance. In short, leave the biscuit to the bakers and the rest to us. Straightforward so far?' You looked at your two colleagues. Bowen seemed to be about to interrupt again, but didn't. Lowestoft was looking at his hands and paying close attention to what you were saying. You proceeded.

'The important thing is that . . .'

Suddenly you wanted a drink. More than anything. Your mouth had gone dry; you swallowed but there was nothing there. On the desk stood a jug of water – it rattled against the rim of the glass when you poured. A little spilled out. But you kept talking. On the ball as ever.

'The important thing,' you repeated, raising the glass to your mouth. The three of them were watching: you sat at your desk holding the glass to your lips.

If only you could have opened the window for longer – it seemed to be getting even hotter. There was sweat on your brow, on your palms. You took a small sip – then another – slowly, gently. They would have to wait for you. You tried to swallow. There was water in your mouth now, but your throat wouldn't engage. You could feel a small trickle beginning to run down at the side. Carefully you reached to wipe it away with the back of your hand – your free hand. You put down the glass. Then, having finally managed to swallow, you wiped your lips again and repeated into yourself: 'The important thing is,' – a silent rehearsal before continuing aloud: 'The important thing is to keep in mind what Turner once said to us: "We must never forget that we are selling biscuits." Remember?' You paused, then glanced at each of your audience in turn before proceeding: 'Biscuits, note – not colours, typeface and the rest.'

More water.

'No one's arguing with that,' Bowen said abruptly.

'I think what Morris is trying to get at is . . .'

Lowestoft looked at you questioningly.

You motioned slightly with your hand to stop him – you could explain yourself quite well enough. You were speaking clearly now, and with confidence.

'We are divided into separate parts,' you continued. 'Design. Sales. Promotion. Research. And so forth. Each more or less autonomous, and yet with one aim in common: to sell biscuits. Majestic biscuits.'

'Come on, Morris,' Bowen began.

Another drink of water.

'But,' you looked at him, 'but that is simply not the case at all, is it? We forget we're selling biscuits. We hardly ever see a biscuit, do we? Any of us. Do you eat Majestics at home? No, and neither do I—'

'Morris,' interrupted Bowen firmly. 'You carried yesterday's meeting. Well done. And because of that I'm a very busy man today, a very busy man. I've got a great deal of work to redo. I haven't time to sit here and be lectured at. If you've got something to say then say it.'

'And that's just the point,' you explained eagerly, sitting forward in your seat. 'That is just the point. All we're interested in is who will carry the meeting. Am I going to win? Is he going to win? A whole lot of separate departments fighting with each other when we should be on the same side. We *are* on the same side.'

'I'm off.' Bowen stood up.

'Listen, Larry. I'm not getting at you—'

'You're not getting at anything, Morris. And I've got a lot of work to do. Bye, Dan.' He left.

Lowestoft then said something to Katherine; she also got up and left. There were just the two of you now.

'What I want to—' you began, but Lowestoft interrupted.

'It's not that I disagree with you, Morris. You've got a point there. A good point, in fact. But considering the circumstances, hardly one to call a meeting for. You really put him through it yesterday – and he took it. He saw the sense of what you had to say and let you overrule him. Not many would have been so reasonable.'

'It's exactly what—'

'Let me finish, Morris,' Lowestoft continued. 'That was yesterday. This is different.'

More water.

But there was none in the glass.

You needed to open the window. You needed more water. You needed to stand up and open the window for some fresh air. You needed to pour more water into the glass. Lowestoft was still talking. You stood up, slid the window open again.

The lorry had driven away from the loading bay, and the men were now enjoying a rest before the next one appeared. Suddenly, as you watched them, you remembered the foreman telling you they called it 'a full house' when the exact number of boxes on the trolleys had filled a lorry. The trolleys opposite were all empty. You wanted to turn and interrupt Lowestoft's flow of well-intentioned platitudes with the phrase 'A full house', then point out of the window. All he would have seen, of course, was a few men leaning against trolleys, but in reality you knew the whole scene was charged with greater significance: A full house. You wanted to explain this to him, to let him know something about the real workers at Majestic's, to open his eyes a bit. You knew what was going on, you were still in touch with the real world. The foreman was called Stan – and on the days when you drove to the office you usually gave him a wave as you parked the car. Though it was many years since you had spent that first week there, he remembered you all right.

You sat down. Lowestoft was still talking, and you still wanted a drink. But not water this time – unless it was *aqua vitae*. And some Schubert. Or possibly something less romantic – a Haydn symphony? No, you decided you would rather have something clear, light and sunny: the Dvorak wind serenade. Dvorak and Courvoisier. What syllables! Dvorak and Courvoisier.

'Well, Morris?' Lowestoft had concluded at last.

'Fine, fine – I'm fine,' you replied.

He was looking at you closely.

'Everything's fine, Dan,' you reassured him. Then you said more slowly, 'Really, no problem,' and met his gaze.

It was time to stand up, you realised. Time to shake hands and show him the door.

'Morris, I think you should go home,' he urged.

He got to his feet – now you only had to steer him in the right direction.

Lowestoft continued: 'You've been overdoing it a bit recently. Why not take—?'

'I'm fine. A good meeting yesterday, wasn't it?'

'Yes, but—'

'Well, then? I'm fine, I tell you. I've enough work and enough energy to keep me going until—'

'That's not the point, Morris.'

You started walking towards the door, knowing he would follow.

'I'm fine, Dan. Believe me.'

A moment's pause. Then a serious and sincere look.

'Thanks for your concern,' you added. Thanks and goodbye. Almost there.

'Okay, Morris, okay. If you feel that – But remember, if you need—'

'Sure.'

A handshake, and he was in the corridor.

'I'll look after myself. Don't worry about me – concentrate on the biscuits!'

94

'Goodbye, Morris.'

'Bye, Dan,' giving him a see-you-again-soon smile.

You closed the door. Time for the immaculate and invisible ocean. For Dvorak and Courvoisier. You could sit and watch the men load the next lorry while drinking to a full house.

A full bottle for a full house.

The lights were on in the loading bay and Dvorak was done. Long done. You were going to be home late. Not yet, however. You weren't home yet. But you would be – when you were. When you were – then you would be. Late. Not as in dead but as in dead-drunk. Dead-drunk, late sober. That's what you would be: not late and drunk, but late sober.

Would Mary have understood that? She understands everything else. But understanding's not enough, is it? (Though she doesn't understand *that*.) Nor love either. Nothing is enough – that's all. All and nothing. When one drink is too much the rest are never enough. Never.

No longer a full bottle either. Nor full marks. You remembered: in some exams at school you'd start off with full marks, with twenty points, and each time you made a mistake you lost a mark. You were given twenty points and the chance to lose them twenty times over. That's what it felt like: twenty points when you were born – and in no time at all they marked you down to next to nothing. Like themselves.

These days you've forgotten you ever had anything more, and expect nothing better.

But sometimes, especially when you're drunk, you remember what it was like to have full marks, and to lose them. Then, instead of remaining at near-zero as usual, you hammer straight through into the negatives. Hard drinking is hard work, but you keep at it. Practice makes imperfect. That evening as you sat in your office with Dvorak and Courvoisier you must have reached minus twenty. At least. You could feel the sense of loss as never before. You seemed to be going further and further away – but from what? You had no idea; only that the more you drank, the harder, the more painful it became; and that the distance seemed to measure the grief you felt. But – grief about what? Again you had no idea. It hurt, though. Terribly. And so—

Coat. Closing the office door and out through the open-plan, the lift, the plate-glass doors, the drive and the main gate.

The off-licence just in case. Just *a* case, you nearly said to the man, almost laughing aloud. Then down the narrow lane towards the station without touching the path, but holding the brick wall steady on the one side and the metal railing on the other.

The platform. The train empty enough to toast absent friends.

Then home. The light on in the bedroom. Unlock the door and up a flight of stairs that buckled from side to side in the summer evening heat. Towards a door smeared with colour sliding over and over: that familiar TV screen, the horizontal hold gone.

96

The ceiling slowly starting to carousel.

Mary?

She was already in bed.

'Are you all right, Morris?' she asked.

Of course you were all right. A kiss would prove that heaven and hell were in the same place, you tried to tell her. You kissed her. Then talked about love for ten minutes, holding her so tightly the bed spilled you on to the floor.

Steadying the ground, your feet apart like standing on the centre of a see-saw. Not moving forward, but balancing the room exactly as it was. When Mary sat up, you took a step backwards to compensate, and at the same time held your hand out towards her to give her reassurance.

'Sallright, Mary,' you told her. 'Easy does it.'

Never had you sensed so fully the nature of balance – and the balance of nature, you said aloud – that holds everything together. An inattentive gesture or remark could have brought down the whole building, or, at the very least, cracked the walls from side to side. Never had you had so much confidence in your ability to hold all this together: as if you had reached out and were touching everything in the world at once.

You stood utterly still; in the distance a train whistled.

'Even that,' you said to her, 'even that is part of what I feel for you.'

'Morris?' she began.

But you wanted to explain how everyone started life with twenty points – and now that you had reached minus twenty, only the minus sign was keeping you from full marks. If you could erase the minus sign, you told her, you would have full marks once again. It was so simple, so very simple, you insisted.

'Come to bed,' she urged.

She was being understanding. All at once you felt that sense of loss, that terrible grief returning.

Mary folded back the sheet.

'Please, Morris, come to bed.'

Finally you undressed and got in beside her. For a few moments you lay quite still. She would probably expect you to put your arm around her, so you did. But she didn't move.

'Do you want the light off?' she asked.

More understanding.

You didn't answer. Instead, you slipped the shoulder-strap of her nightdress down, you began to brush the skin lightly with the tips of your fingers: backwards and forwards, while pressing yourself against her.

'You feel nice.' You kissed her cheek. Her hair tickled your face slightly – and when you turned away the room turned slowly with you.

Sliding her nightdress lower at the front, you began to stroke her breasts. You were feeling very drunk. Then to kiss them. You grew more excited every moment, and imagined being inside her, thrusting as hard as possible. You licked each nipple in turn, then slid your hand down her body in a long slow caress.

Still she didn't move. You paused, keeping your hand where it was. Was she angry? Bored? You had no idea. You were unsure about going any further, yet unwilling to stop completely and turn over. You tried to see the expression on her face, but were afraid to meet her eyes. You held your breath; then several moments later her legs parted, and you relaxed.

You began pressing yourself even closer to her, your fingers moving inside her.

'Is it good?' you whispered.

'Yes,' she answered. Her breathing had become louder.

A moment later she grasped your prick – but despite the desire that filled you, it was quite soft. You could feel her stroking it, pulling it, drawing back the foreskin – trying to coax some life into it. She kissed you, she was encouraging you – doing her best to help you.

Your excitement began to give way to panic. You tried to picture other situations, other women. With her hand on your prick, on its limpness, its uselessness, you imagined her saying, 'Jelly, it's jelly.' But she hadn't; she was still kissing you, and seemed to be dandling your prick like a baby's finger. 'Don't let it go,' you thought to yourself, 'or you mightn't be able to find it again,' you almost laughed aloud. You continued caressing her breasts and stroking inside her as though trying to rediscover your desire somewhere in her body. You knew that whatever you said or did was of no real importance, however, for everything had come down to the simple fact that you could not get hard. Nor even pretend to. In your desperation you felt each caress she gave as a punishment for not responding.

Then all at once you realised you had begun to stiffen. She continued rubbing your prick.

'Mary . . .' you said. She was hurting you.

'Yes – yes,' she urged.

She was rubbing it from the tip down to the base, pulling roughly.

'Yes, Morris, yes – that's good.'

Your prick was quite erect now, but immediately she'd spoken you could sense it faltering.

'No,' you protested, 'don't . . . '

'Don't what?'

'Don't – don't praise me,' you managed to say.

'What do you mean, Morris?' Momentarily her hand stopped.

No more understanding. You didn't want that. It felt like theft. By being understanding she robbed you of what you really were. Already your prick had begun to slacken.

'Mary,' you whispered. 'Take me as I am – just as I am.'

No understanding, you told her, no hoping – nothing, just you. The drunkness, the fear, the cowardice.

'No, Morris, no,' she interrupted. 'You're not like that. No.'

But you couldn't stop now. You were confessing to the pain. As you spoke you felt as if, piece by piece, you were being relieved of a great burden, the need to pretend to her – and to yourself. There was a sense of overwhelming release, the possibility of rest.

'No, no,' she insisted. 'You're not like that – you mustn't believe it. I know that's not true. You're good, Morris, you really are.'

She continued caressing you, kissing you, holding you close – her voice soothing, comforting.

But you longed for her to dig her nails into your

skin – making you draw breath at the sudden pain – to let the poison out, the self-disgust.

She was trying to calm you, stroking your hair, saying it didn't matter. Nothing mattered so long as you loved her and she loved you – *that* was the most important thing, she said. She kept repeating the word 'love' over and over again.

If only she could have clawed her way into you, reached to the suffering deep inside, to touch it, to accept. Only that pain could have affirmed what you were then – not her words and caresses, her love without action.

'Mary,' you began, 'it's not just love – that's at the beginning, the easy part. It's the rest as well, the—'

But all at once you knew you were going to be sick. Violently you wrenched yourself out of her grasp and turned just in time, spraying vomit on to the edge of the blankets and the floor.

For several moments you hung over the edge of the bed.

A basin appeared.

'I got that for the carpet, not for you,' Mary stated, then left the room, slamming the door behind her.

You remained staring down into the basin, into the mess of colours, breathing in the stink and being sick until there was no more sick to come. Afterwards you lay back on the bed, exhausted.

She might at least have switched off the light on her way out, you thought to yourself, but didn't laugh. Instead you pulled the sheet up to cover your face, closed your eyes and hoped you'd soon pass out. You wanted to cry, but couldn't. Not alone.

9

Next morning was beautiful. No hangover. A gift. You woke a few minutes before the alarm clock, so with a pat on the head you sent it back to sleep. Then, lying wonderfully at peace, you let sunlight flood into the room to colour everything naturally – even the extravagance of Mary's Japanese dressing gown. She, also, was still asleep, but a pat on the head would have woken her, so, gently, ever so gently, you raised yourself up from the pillows and eased yourself out from under the blankets. Inch at a time, gradually modulating horizontal into vertical. Then you saw the basin.

A clean basin stood at the side of the bed. You couldn't remember putting it there. You looked at it again. The usual basin. At least you hadn't been sick: it was still clean. You couldn't remember much after coming home, except that it was late and Mary was already in bed. You'd been at endless meetings to rethink the new wrapper, followed by some desk-work. Hardly a memorable evening. You must have felt sick though – and brought the basin on your way from the kitchen. Luckily you hadn't needed it. You felt fine now. A false alarm. No need to false-alarm Mary, however, so you decided you would take the basin with you when you went downstairs.

Your clothes seemed to be cascading imperceptibly from the back of the chair on to the floor. Let them, you thought. They looked tired and rejected – so you rejected them. Something new instead for a new morning. Something fresh, clean and crisp; something light. But quietly – you didn't want to waken Mary – and so, nothing too crisp.

Sliding open the sock and underwear drawer, the shirt drawer, the wardrobe door – but ever so carefully, silently, smoothly. Which suit? A suit to suit the day, of course. To mediate between the day outside you and the day inside you, complementing both. The light blue, you decided. Discreet, but partaking of deep joy.

Grasping the basin in one hand, you closed the bedroom door with an all-but-silenced click, then off down the stairs two at a time. Not too fast, however, not until the landing. One step. Two step. Three step. And four and five and six then turn. Seven, nine, eleven, all the way to the bottom.

Into the kitchen. The basin back where it belonged. Then on with the tea, the toast and Mozart. A beautiful morning. You opened the back door and breathed: a beautiful day. The birds were singing, the trees were rustling with pleasure, the flowers were growing, scenting and colouring. The bushes, the stone wall, the sky. Ah, the sky! Another deep breath and back to the toast.

The table was set, and you were set to call them down. Cups and plates, spoons and bowls. Hurry – you told them to hurry to see the garden, hurry to hear the birds – hurry to breathe and live.

The table looked good, the tea was perfect (and there was extra water on in case). There was marmalade, honey, butter, jam and Shreddies. A feast. You called them to the feast. There was toast, cool fresh milk, and . . .

And in they came! You welcomed them: Good morning, a chair for Elise; a chair for Tom; a chair for Mary, your good wife. Then last, but not least, a chair for yourself. All together now. A family breakfast. A family feast.

Smiles and hot buttered toast. Four brimming cups; lemon for Mary. Perfect, perfect. Three sleepy faces, three very yawny mouths. The garden was still bright, the tea was delicious, and Mozart was – Mozart! Piano concerto number two, written when he was ten, more than two hundred years old and as good that morning as—

'You can't get on the radio when you're ten,' interrupted young Tom.

'Of course you can,' you laughed.

'Will I?' he asked.

'If you write music as good as that, you will,' you replied, then hummed along with it for a moment, conducting a few bars with the butter-knife. 'Wait for the rondo – a real belter!'

'It's boring,' stated Elise.

'Boring?' you repeated with mock-incredulity.

'And too loud,' said Mary. She reached over and turned it down. That was the first time she had spoken since coming downstairs. That was her morning greeting.

You sat very still for a moment, then drank some tea. You had got up early to make breakfast for everyone – a surprise. And that was all she had to say: 'The music's too loud.' You drank some more tea. The garden was outside, and the sky. Sunlight. She was tired, that was all. You smiled at her. Three minutes passed. The rondo.

Mozart was to be succeeded by his son, you were told. The announcer's little joke – although some say Francis Xavier's true father was Sussmeyer, Mozart's pupil, the one who finished the Requiem. You had never heard anything by the son. It should be interesting, you thought. Mary was talking with Tom about his swimming class and the visit to their granny's that evening. Elise wanted some orange juice. Francis Xavier Mozart had over forty opus numbers, it seemed. He was neglected nowadays. A piano trio. A minute passed, and you thought to yourself: 'Justly neglected.'

Then ten minutes passed, and breakfast was over.

You announced to Mary that there was something you would like to show her. It was the wrong time; you knew that she was angry, but you were leading her into the garden. You wanted to put your arms around her and tell her that you loved her. You knew it was the wrong time.

A patio, you remarked. What did she think about having a patio where the family could eat outdoors on summer evenings?

'I could move the shed to the top corner,' you suggested, 'and lay some paving stones, or whatever the crazy ones are called. From the french windows over to the beginning of the lawn.'

Mary said nothing. She stood beside the back door. You talked on, developing the proposed renovations: an all-weather table with four chairs and an extra two, foldaway, in case of guests. What would be the best colour? you asked her. A martini-style umbrella in the middle? An extension socket set into the side wall for a light perhaps, not too strong, of course, fixed in position above the—

Without a word, Mary went back into the house. Although you knew it would only make things worse, you followed her.

'What's wrong with you?' you demanded.

She glared back at you but said nothing.

'I said – what's wrong with you?'

She had turned to leave the kitchen. You reached out and grabbed her arm.

'Let go,' she said firmly.

'I asked you a question.'

'And?'

'And I want an answer,' you insisted.

'Well, then, you'll just have to want,' she replied, and turned away. She went into the hall, where she called Tom and Elise.

For several moments you remained standing in the kitchen, then followed her. She was opening the front door. Tom must have already gone out; Elise turned to wave goodbye. In a moment the house would be empty apart from you standing there, isolated.

'Mary,' you began.

'This evening, Morris.' Pulling the door behind her, she added: 'If you're home, and if you're not too drunk, that is.'

You listened to them walk down the steps and along the gravel path. Then came the slam of the car doors, the engine starting, Mary driving off.

For nearly a minute you stood in the centre of the hall,

then returned to the kitchen where you picked up your briefcase, locked the back door, and switched off the radio. It was time to go.

You arrived at the station a few minutes early, eight seventeen for eight twenty-three, so you walked the length of the platform and back; then sat down by the chocolate machines. A glance at the empty sky. A look down the tracks, at the fence posts, the trespass-notice, the timetable. A man in a white jersey and jeans asked you the time. You told him. A dizzying perfume: a woman with red shoes walked past. A man with grey sleepy eyes. A red-faced man, swollen.

At the sound of the train entering the station you turned and saw a piece of white paper flutter briefly in front of the driver's window. For a split second you thought of the cottage you had lived in as a child, its white walls – then the train stopped abruptly. Only halfway into the station.

The driver has dashed out of his cab on to the platform a few feet from you.

He shouts, 'I've killed someone! I've killed someone!' – and rushes back into his cab again.

Through his open window you can hear him scream into his radio: 'I've killed someone! I've killed someone!' He looks like a man drowning – his arms threshing wildly, his mouth wide open, his eyes staring out through the glass.

The passengers have leant out of the windows or opened the carriage doors to see what is happening. Those who were about to board have moved to the platform's edge and are looking down to see as best they can; or else, having looked, turn away immediately afterwards from the mess of colours crumpled under the wheels. You stare at it. A complete stranger addresses you – you nod and keep staring. The complete stranger addresses someone else. The three of you stare down at the remains of the man with the white jersey and jeans. At the mess of colours. Less than a minute ago he had been standing beside you. He had asked you the time. He is much further away now than you can even begin to understand.

Another stranger addresses you. Everyone feels the need to talk, to say something to someone. You can feel it all around you and inside you. A kind of panic because you also want to talk, to touch people.

The driver stands at the side of the engine. He is young, hardly even your age. A man is holding him by the arm just above the elbow, as though to support him. On the driver's other side a man and a woman are talking excitedly. You catch the odd phrase: 'So quick, so quick.' The driver is repeating his version and shaking his head. He is being forgiven, excused, held, and then listened to. Forgiven, excused, held, and then listened to all over again.

You go backwards and forwards between the sight of the dead man under the train and the activity round the driver – trying to make sense of what has happened. Although you had never seen the man in the white jersey before, you feel that you should be upset. Nearby a woman is crying.

The other passengers have begun to drift away, to make new arrangements for their journey. People stand in small groups discussing the availability of taxis, buses – or how long it might be before the trains are running again. Can the points be operated so that the trains in both directions use the other platform?

You feel a strong pull to join one of these groups: the taxi-crowd, the other-platformers, the forgivers. They appear to understand what has happened. By yourself, however, you simply keep blundering from the dead man to the driver and back again – as along the critical distance, suddenly revealed, between the past and the present, trying desperately to decide where you belong. Backwards and forwards you go, bewildered by what, in your state of shock, appears as two aspects of the same person: one dead, and the other still crying aloud his guilt. Eventually someone asks you if you'd like to make up the number for a taxi.

You look back just as you are about to leave the platform: the train is at rest half in and half out of the station, giving the scene a very static quality. Like a photograph. To a casual glance there would seem to be nothing unusual: this is the train entering the station, and these are the waiting passengers. You, however, possess another and more sinister interpretation – and for a brief moment as you pause at the ticket barrier you feel the need to return and reassure yourself of what has happened. To touch the metal front of the engine; to see again the body lying underneath the wheels. You want to be quite certain that the tragic element, which at this distance you can only sense, does not come from you nor in any way belongs to you; that in this case your nature is quite innocent of any—

'Come on!' calls the man. 'The taxi is waiting.'

You turn and go to join him.

The sun was shining into your little mud-cramped, mud-trap office. So brightly that you could not bear to look out of the window. Instead, you stared at the multicoloured graphs, the Mondrian, and the blue-backed files. Suddenly Katherine's back was towards you. She was leaving the room. Abruptly. Angrily.

A moment ago you had put your hand up her skirt, and now she is storming off towards the door. The dictation pad still in her hand.

She had been standing beside you, close beside you, leaning over to indicate a difficulty in one of the letters that had arrived. Her fingertip was tracing the line:

'Respecting the delivery date, we would consider that—'

'Shouldn't there actually be a date mentioned?' she had asked.

Her fingernail was pressed against the comma where she felt the date should be, and so lightly pressed that you could hardly believe she wasn't in fact touching you.

'Here, d'you mean, Katherine?' you had suggested, pointing directly to the comma as well, your finger almost grazing hers.

'Yes, and here too,' she indicated a similar omission in another line further down the letter. This time your fingers touched.

'And over,' she added, reaching to turn the page, her palm and the back of your hand making brief contact. Your left hand was resting on the arm of your executive swivel, and gradually the chair turned until the back of your hand was against her leg. She did not move away.

'And lastly,' she continued, 'where it says something about penalty clauses . . . ' You let your hand rise ever so slightly from the arm of your chair, keeping it in contact, in gentle contact, with her leg. The touch of her skin on the back of your hand. The hem of her skirt. She still hadn't moved; she was expecting you to—

'Katherine!' you call after her. But already everything is happening somewhere inside you, even her crying on your shoulder while you reassure her, telling her how this and how that. You need only act it out: say the words, perform the gestures – and she, in turn, will play her part.

And so, almost laughing aloud at the simplicity of things, you get up from your chair.

'Katherine,' you repeat, taking her arm.

You will turn her round, and she will be angry and in tears. You will comfort her, telling her how much she means to you and has meant ever since you first met. That first morning at the lift, just after she had started to work here, does she remember? you will ask You will turn her face round so you can see the tears, and be so deeply moved as to take her in your arms, then begin stroking her hair.

Your hand is on her arm: 'Katherine, I—'

She faces you. She is almost in tears. You have not let go of her arm, however.

'Katherine,' you try again, 'you must understand that—'

'How could you?' She is trembling.

'It was—'

'No, no,' she is looking away from you. 'What were you—?' she begins slowly. 'What did you think that I—?'

'Katherine.' You have moved a half-step closer to her.

'And let go my arm,' she pleads.

Her face is very pale. She glares at you – standing only a few inches away.

Although you know it is only going to make things worse, you move slightly to put your arm around her shoulder, to pull her towards you, to comfort her.

'Listen, Katherine, I know how you must feel. I'm very sorry that . . . '

You speak slowly and deliberately to show that you are deeply moved. You hesitate briefly before continuing.

'But is it really so unlikely that—?'

'You. Say. Nothing.' Her voice is suddenly firm. She pauses between each word as if with the effort required to utter the next. 'Nothing.'

She steps backwards from you.

'And don't touch me again. Ever,' she adds, then pauses uncertainly. 'You bastard.'

As she says the word 'bastard', you notice that her voice trembles momentarily. Soon she will be in tears – and then you can draw towards her and comfort her.

You continue your previous sentence as though you had been anticipating her interruption and that, in fact, everything was all right.

'Is it really so unlikely,' you proceed, 'that I should feel like this for you?'

For a moment she stares at you, but says nothing. A good sign. She doesn't believe you, of course. She is surprised – but as she has said nothing you keep talking.

'It's just . . . ' you turn a little to one side, slightly embarrassed. 'It's just that everything's come out wrong, Katherine.'

You look into her eyes now; you are being sincere.

'I did not want it like this. Not like this,' you repeat with regret, holding up your hand against any interruption. You want to be truly honest now.

'I didn't mean it like this,' you speak almost sorrowfully, but as though you were making great efforts not to betray that sorrow – for you are too ashamed.

She still doesn't believe you – but she is listening. Now you tell her about what she meant to you, 'even when we met that first morning in the lift,' you say. Does she remember?

She nods, but says nothing.

You continue: you would notice and chat to her in the open-plan; then she became your secretary. How hard it has been, you tell her, having her so close day after day – and yet being unable to say anything. But how much harder it would have been without her. Does she understand what you mean?

So many times you have almost begun to tell her, to say something that would allow you to . . . Here you make a vague gesture instead of completing the sentence. But either the phone would ring, you explain, or someone would interrupt, or – and here you look away briefly – you just couldn't.

You give particular examples.

You continue: every time your fingers touched when passing letters for signature it was as though – and she is still listening – as though . . .

You leave this sentence unfinished also, and lay your hand gently on her shoulder.

'It's been very hard, Katherine, very hard,' you repeat, slowly, looking directly into her face.

'And now it's all come out, all at once – and all wrong.'

You pause; then in a concerned tone you ask:

'Do you understand?'

You pause again. Then apply a very slight pressure on her shoulder before you move your hand in preparation for replacing it nearer her neck.

Then you ask: 'Can you understand, Katherine? Can you see what I mean?' You are speaking very slowly, carefully – sincerely.

She looks back at you in silence. Confused.

'Oh, Katherine, Katherine,' you say in a hardly audible voice – as if you did not want her to hear you speak her name in this way. The slightest pressure now will draw her towards you. There is no need to say anything more. In a few seconds you will be able to put your arm around her.

It is very quiet in your office: you and Katherine stand close together for several moments, facing each other without speaking.

Over her shoulder you can see three lorries at the loading bay opposite. The checker is sitting on an empty box at the side with his clipboard, marking off the different kinds of biscuit as they are loaded. From this distance it is difficult to see exactly when he marks the paper. He is talking to one of the men who leans against an empty trolley – perhaps one of the lorries has just been filled and they are waiting for it to drive off.

You begin very, very gently to stroke Katherine's hair. She does not pull away. When you hear the sound of a lorry starting up, you let the stroking of her hair become briefly the caressing of her cheek. Then almost immediately you step back a little from her and place both your hands on her shoulders. You smile now – not joyfully, but rather as one friend might smile to another.

'All right?' you ask softly. Affectionately.

She smiles back, rather shyly at first, but then with more confidence. You want to kiss her now, but know it is too soon. Instead you draw her towards you, and, though hardly touching her, brush her forehead with your lips.

You slide your arm around her back to give a tender, deeply-felt hug. She does not pull away – and you know you can relax.

It is after three o'clock – time when you usually partake of the immaculate and invisible ocean. Some brandy and Bach, you'd planned on earlier; but instead you are sitting, staring straight ahead at that part of the wall where the productivity charts hang. From outside you can hear the lorries and the shouts of the men. But you do not turn your chair as usual to face the window and look up into the sky, into the clear waters. Are you aware of how anxious, how frightened you are?

Katherine believed you. You held her in your arms until she believed every word you said. A success. Another one. Since she left the room, however, you have been staring straight ahead and holding on to the noise coming from outside. With all your strength. As though your life depended upon it.

As you listen you keep trying to imagine the loading bay, the lorries, the car park, and the other buildings outside – trying to picture them in your mind, to fix them there. To be *certain* of them. You close your eyes, concentrating harder and harder.

Unable to relax even for one second, you check off each familiar detail: the car park, the loading bay, the trolleys, the large wooden doors, the slate roof, the colour of the sky, the white clouds. But whenever you reach the colour white you stop and have to begin all over again. Everything must be included, and in the correct order, or – or what? You have no idea.

You begin again: the car park, the loading bay, the trolleys, the large wooden doors . . .

Suddenly you have got up from your chair and gone out of the room, passing Katherine's desk – but she is not there. Then straight through the typing pool. No one pays any attention as you walk down the aisle between two rows of clattering machines, bent heads; then past the potted plants, the coat-hooks, and out into the corridor.

The lift is on the ground floor, and so you press the call-button. You wait for a few seconds and again press the call-button. A few seconds later you have gone further down the corridor and taken the stairs.

Three flights to the bottom, two steps at a time, then along another corridor with two waiting areas: curtains, easy chairs, low tables and magazines. Through the large glass doors and outside.

Fresh air. A deep breath. Briefly you stand on the steps. One of the two men who pass greets you, but you pay no attention. The glass door shuts after him. You remain on the step, staring at the cars lined up in the car park.

You walk in the direction of the loading bay. There are two lorries parked, and several men wearing overalls. The sun is shining – one of the men is stripped to the waist, he is very tanned. The men are shouting at each other. You approach them. Reggae music comes from a radio propped against one of the posts. You are about ten feet away when the youngest, a youth with his hair cropped very short, notices you. He looks aggressive.

There are no steps leading up to the loading bay – you remember that they are at the side. It feels as though you are walking on the bed of a shallow harbour between large lorry-ships, looking up at the men standing on the quayside.

Crop-head calls out 'Stan!' then nods in your direction.

An older man carrying papers and a clipboard comes round from the back of one of the lorries. You recognise him as the foreman from that first week; he stands at the edge of the quayside and looks down at you.

'Problem, is there?' he asks.

No friendly greeting – doesn't he know you?

You don't reply soon enough, and, as it seems possible that you might not have heard what he said, he turns to crop-head: 'Turn it off, Barry.'

The radio is switched off. Silence.

You remain standing still, glancing first at the older man, then at the others who by now have all approached the edge of the quay.

'Is there something needing done?' Stan asks politely. 'We're almost through with the loading.'

Still, however, you don't answer. Your arms are at your sides, your hands clenched. You are breathing heavily. Stan has given you an encouraging look: he is trying to find out what you want.

'If there's anything . . . ?' he prompts again.

Your right hand clenches tighter. You are about to take a step towards the quayside, but don't. You remain silent.

Suddenly the crop-headed youth laughs. The older men have begun to grin at each other. Stan glares fiercely at crop-head.

'You!' you call out suddenly, pointing at the youth. Your arm is trembling. 'You!' you repeat loudly. 'What do you know about—?' then stop uncertainly. 'About—? About . . . ?' But you are unable to finish the sentence.

Crop-head stops laughing instantly, and looks over to the foreman.

'Don't – don't you dare laugh,' you continue, shouting – and take two steps towards him. You are very angry.

'Don't you dare,' you repeat at the top of your voice. Your arm is shaking, but you manage to keep it pointing at the boy – emphasising each word with your finger: 'Don't. You. Dare. Laugh.'

For a moment no one moves. You keep your arm outstretched. Then abruptly you let it drop, turn, and walk away.

A few seconds later you can hear the boy saying: 'I didn't mean anything, Stan, honest. I didn't.' But you are walking quickly and do not hear the foreman's reply.

Halfway across the car park you look up at the main office building for a few minutes, trying to work out which is your window. A car has to sound its horn to get you to move out of the way. Then you continue. You go through the glass doors, take the lift the three floors to your office, where you turn the executive swivel round to face the ocean, reach into the drawer for a three-quarters full bottle of brandy, and put on the headphones. Beethoven's *Missa Solemnis*.

The descending solo violin introduction to the Benedictus was filling everything inside you. A stroll in the evening air after dinner, you thought to yourself. Yes, Mary might well suggest a stroll in the evening air. Not too far; to the park and back again. A matter of fifteen minutes at the most, after which you would return home to spend the rest of the evening quietly together. Conversation, listening to music, reading, TV or whatever.

The Benedictus was growing louder. There was the taste of brandy, its reassurance; and then the creak of your executive chair-back as you heaved yourself laboriously to your feet.

A fifteen-minute stroll, a breath of fresh air, a look at the night sky before—

At the last minute you have steadied yourself against a small shelf beside the filing cabinet.

You pause for a moment, but the shelf is giving way under your weight.

There is the sensation of falling.

You grasp at the books and files on the small shelf, and then at the papers stacked there.

You grasp at the top of the metal cabinet, then the metal handles, then the soft blue carpet you are lying on now.

Falling into a silence that presses down harder and harder. That reaches into you: your eyes that can't stay open, your mouth's saliva.

Silence. Tape hiss. Time to go home. A refreshing siesta and now it's time to go home, to replace the cassette, the books, the files and papers. A tidy-up at the end of the day. Four forty-five. Time to recatalogue the brandy and the glass. A glance out the window, straighten the tie and dust off the suit. To go home. To Mary. The accusations are at her mother's this evening. Just the two of you. All this evening.

A surprise dinner then. Cooked by yourself. All your own work. You, and a couple of Corbieres to set it off. Or else a Beaujolais, perhaps.

Coat, open-plan, goodbye, the lift, potted plants and low tables, the plate-glass door, the main gate, the lane, the station.

Where the colour white flutters briefly as the train comes in.

Six stops. The walk. The off-licence, the butcher, baker, veg, the front door, the key and in.

The biscuit-day done, you've come home thinking what the hell. Dinner. But first things first: pick a toe-tapping Haydn quartet, chambré the wine, sharpen the veg knife to an Opus 33. Mary will be home soon – so move into overdrive.

You're well into the *largo* and reaching down for the mixed herbs when suddenly it begins to snow. Just a few flakes. You stand up straight again, stretch out your hand, and sure enough a few crystals lie there briefly. You taste them. Snow. The real thing. Melting on your palm.

The rondo is just finishing when the doorbell rings. The doorbell rings again. It is Mary.

'The key was in the lock,' she states.

You tell her she is looking very lovely, especially with her hair brushed back so differently. 'Hairdresser?' you ask.

'You left the key in the lock,' she insists.

'A surprise. A dinner-surprise,' you announce. And smile.

'But—?' She's puzzled.

You smile: 'We don't need explanations, but wine.'

You give her a glass.

'And music.'

You turn over the record and drink to surprises. Then to dinner-surprises.

You take her glass and place it on the sideboard.

Your left hand in her right you lead the dance into a brisk allegro.

She turns down the gas. She wants to help? Fine. As you wish to slip into something more comfortable you suggest she has another drink and stirs a pot or two.

You won't be long. You smile.

Up the stairs three at a time. A quick burst of the Mass in B minor – the Gloria – to get yourself ready. Then it's off with the day-clothes and into the en-suite for a shave and splash. And to finish – on with cologne and the informal evening wear.

But first you turn up Bach to sing along.

With the biscuits behind you it's good to come home. The accusations gone, Mary downstairs, the dinner on – and Bach. You are filled with the sensations of soap, heat, steel, plastic, pastel colours, strip-lighting and your own reflection.

Into whatever room's left you cram the sound of choir, soloists and orchestra.

Enough?

You must choose a tie; you knot it well. You fold the collar down neatly.

You run your hand over your smooth cheek.

You turn the Mass up. Up.

You choose two cuff-links and—

'Are you deaf?' asks the woman beside you whose lipstick is suddenly too bright. It is Mary.

'I've been shouting to you for ages. The phone rang and they're waiting for you.'

'Yes, it is a bit loud,' you agree.

You switch the volume down as you pass – and into the emptiness left by the decreasing sound you pull this girl with long black hair.

'Mary . . .' you begin.

'Hurry up, they're waiting for you – on the phone.'

And as you turn, snow begins falling once more. No longer just a few flakes, not now – but everywhere around you the colour white.

You stumble out of the bedroom into the hall, grasping for the banisters. It is an effort to lift and place each foot each time. An effort to feel for each separate stair as you go down, step by step, into the thickly falling snow. Into deepening silence.

You have reached the bottom stair at last: you must rescue yourself, placing each foot each time, taking care not to walk in larger and larger circles. Your namesake, you almost laugh aloud, has already circumnavigated the Earth. You must keep forcing yourself forwards, your hands stretched out in front. If the brandy won't come to the stranded traveller then the stranded traveller, you almost laugh aloud . . .

10

Seven-o-one with sunlight seeping through the curtains. A beautiful summer's day. A radiant green lawn. Red, yellow and pink flowers.

You shower, get dressed: underwear, socks, shirt, waistcoat, trousers, jacket and very shiny shoes.

In the mirror: a forty-a-year man if ever there was one, and well worth your weight in biscuits. You straighten your tie, smooth down your hair and leave, closing the door behind you. Halfway down the stairs you stop and go back to open the bedroom door a little. You will be calling Mary to breakfast in a very short time – so, no need to strain the vocal cords.

Down the stairs again, across the hall and into the kitchen. Locatelli and a very quick Courvoisier to keep the morning mud at bay. Water on for tea, bread under the grill. A glimpse of the outside world. A breath of fresh air. Then back into the kitchen for Courvoisier number two. Next: the plates, the cups, the saucers, the spoons and bowls. A Rossini overture. Make the tea and butter the toast. A last Courvoisier, then call the family down. What timing! Masterful as always.

An hour later you've driven Mary to the station, the accusations to school and yourself to work. To the office and the lovely Katherine.

A quick glance round: the multicoloured charts, Courvoisier, the calendar, Mondrian, your desk. Time for a familiarising swivel before looking at the loading bay. The moment for feeling bad.

The bad moment over.

Another swivel, another Courvoisier, then flick the intercom switch. And smile.

'Good morning out there!'

An unfamiliar voice answers: 'Good morning, Mr Magellan.'

'Good morning,' you reply automatically, then add: 'Where's Katherine?'

'She's off sick today, sir. I'm her replacement. Temporary. Miss Donahue.'

The voice betrays some irritation, possibly at your abruptness.

'Off sick?' you repeat.

'Yes, sir,' Miss Donahue pauses before adding with great deliberation: 'Taken ill.'

'What's wrong with her?' you ask.

'I don't know, sir. I'm temporary, that's all.'

Too embarrassed to come in, perhaps, after yesterday's 'romantic' misunderstanding, you wonder. Or else ... ?

'That's all right, Miss Donahue. Never mind. Could you come through in a few minutes, please?'

'Very good, sir.'

You get up from your desk and go to look out of the window. Perhaps she's complained. But no: there was nothing wrong. Nothing. Not really. You didn't do anything wrong. It had been true. Everything you said to her. But it had come out all at once. You held her, told her your feelings. Your true feelings. It's all right. She understood. She believed you.

A Courvoisier while standing back from the window and staring at each of the vast biscuit tins in turn, reading each time the large letters:

The Majestic Baking Co. Ltd.

There are seven biscuit tins, eight including this one. The telephone rings: 'Morning, Morris.' It is Lowestoft.

Some biscuit-banter. An arrangement to meet for lunch.

You have begun glancing through the letters in the in-tray when Miss Donahue comes into the office.

At once you get to your feet to welcome her, and to apologise for any sharpness in your manner over the phone.

'A bit set in my ways,' you explain with a laugh. 'Too early in the day. The sound of an unfamiliar voice . . .'

You complete the sentence with a vague gesture and a smile.

She relaxes. You smile at her again, and by lunchtime you have worked your way through the letters and a report, through two short meetings, three short phone calls, and four long brandies. Her name is Carol. She enjoys going to discos and lives in a flat with three other girls. At the weekends she sometimes takes a bus into the country.

After lunch there is another meeting, more telephone calls and more letters. Carol plays badminton one evening a week. On Tuesdays. Her boyfriend works on the oilrigs. He's away for two weeks every four but he's not jealous. She has an attractive smile.

You used to think of Mozart as eighteenth-century Muzak and could never understand what all the fuss was about. He seemed charming: like a shallow stream bubbling prettily through a well-planned garden. Clear water, but only a few inches deep. Then one day you heard a modulation into G minor: clear water certainly, but so deep that you sensed you would never touch the bottom. What else could wash away the mud that is choking everything around you this afternoon?

Your office window is wide open and yet you can hardly breathe, your body is sweating. Already you have washed your hands and face several times, but you cannot stop this clamminess from seeping out through your skin. And so – Mozart.

You swivel round and gaze into the almost colourless blue of a summer sky. The ocean, brandy, and a sonata for violin and piano. So fine, so passionate, and yet . . .

Already your mind is wandering. The harder you keep grasping at the music, the more elusive it becomes. The more desperately you try to concentrate, the more your efforts come between you and the sound. You try to become weightless, to let the music support you as water would. As brandy does.

You are thinking about Mary, about Katherine – you are certain she wouldn't complain. A change of key catches your attention. Then the recent meeting, Lowestoft. Each time you become aware that your mind is wandering and chattering, you try to silence it – and that effort, too, drowns out the music.

Carol's hair, her smile, the colour white fluttering in

front of the driver's window, your plan for the weekend, the certainty that Katherine will not complain, the colour white, the noise from the loading bay outside. Eventually there is only the taste of brandy set against your persistent attempt at silence.

You let the tape play right to the end, however, and comment to yourself afterwards, 'That was good.' The mud is still around you – but now you've managed to smear some of it over a Mozart sonata as well.

A brandy-coda and you're ready for a walk to the car park. Goodbye to the open-plan, the lift, the potted plants and low tables. The plate-glass doors, a breath of fresh air, the car park, the sea-green car with its sticky lock. Unstick it. Unlocking the seat-cover smell, the heat smell. Opening the window and switching on. First time. Anchors aweigh and, smoothly, faultlessly, sliding out of port despite an awkward kerb-nudge. Steady as she goes. Saluting the harbour master, then bearing hard to starboard into the main lane of a three-lane stretch, watching the centre lane marker buoys, the lighthouse beacons, the badly parked rocks and reef banks.

Heading homewards: you and Boccherini with the wind behind you. The biscuit-box closed for the day. Full speed ahead: pass one, pass another; port, starboard, and round the desert island. A flotilla leeward. Let them know you're coming: a Boccherini-beat upon the horn, some heavy headlight-Morse, and all's clear.

You're through them, through the small fry heading for home. The world's in your wake and can't catch you up – not now, not ever. Port, starboard, and round another island – almost leaning over for that one.

Soon be there. Flick on the signal light, hard to port, ninety degrees and ease upstream. Mind the natives. A short-cut. A short one-way – never been caught, not yet, not ever – and there's the white cliffs of home. Children on the quayside. Step ashore, an arm round each and hornpipe to the kitchen.

The galley and the galley-slave. A joke, honest. A sea-nymph. A mermaid.

'You're drunk.'

One of the oceanides.

Staggering back against the far wall in mock horror, leaning forward again: towards the tilting galley floor or else the slippery egg-yolk, oil, and a breaking baking-bowl of red, green, yellow across the chequered tiles.

'You're drunk. Watch, Morris, it's all over—'

'Mary,' leaning towards her affectionately. Instead, her Medusa-hair and claws.

'Oh, Morris, Morris.' Repeated sound-waves hammering you against the wall. Then forward once again with feeling – but there's a full tide forcing you back against the shore. To slide on to the sand. The restful sand. Resting there, glancing up at the distant noise, at the sound-waves crashing harmlessly far above you.

Enter the accusations wanting to hornpipe again. You'd like to – but it's far more pleasant on the sandy ocean-floor. Too pleasant to rise.

A sea-shanty instead. You're clapping the off-beat:

Hearts of Oak, Arethusa, full blast. Tom and Elise singing and jigging in time while the Medusa looks on. Doesn't she like music?

Up on your feet to catch the beat, and faster. Keep clapping then tapping it out on pot lids, on sideboards. Young Tom's arm – round and round, Elise – a twirl, now Tom again. Catch the beat and keep it; hammer it on cookers, on fridges, on hands and knees to check the chequered tiles are black-stroke-white from wall to wall, keeping perfect time: a through-bass to dance upon.

Which is fine except for looking up afterwards. Raise your eyes and your stomach rises. Swallow hard. Look down. Keep looking down. The black-stroke-white bending this way and that, arching backwards then forwards as the smell of onion-smear on the cutting board, the heat, the cooking-fat heaviness . . .

'Daddy's being sick.'

You've reached the sink at least. Head above the brandy-sick, the wine-sick. Again.

Rest. Listening to the hall clock strike six.

Hold on to the stainless steel rim. Hold tight. The metal feels cool against your forehead. Rest there. Rest – from the journey, the thirty-four-year journey to reach this one moment's peace.

'Morris – Morris!' The anger, the exhaustion in her voice. The pressure of her hand on your shoulder.

There is no need to say anything. Not yet. Mary is standing far beyond the sense of coolness, of rest. There is no need to go to her, not yet. When you are ready you can reply, but for the moment draw this peace out from the metal and take it as deep into you as you can, let it flood into you.

Her hand has pulled away. 'What the hell do you mean by—? And the kids . . . and—?'

You can feel her voice drawing on other moments, poison-moments. You are tensing and gripping the rim tighter. Can't she see that you—?

As though every moment you've ever lived . . .

Holding tightly on to the sink, as on to the whole kitchen, the house, the surface of the Earth itself . . .

As though letting go the stainless steel would be letting go your only grasp upon the world. Can't she see that everything depends upon . . . ?

Suddenly she's turned and walked out of the kitchen, taking Tom and Elise with her. You cannot go after her, nor go away. Every moment you have ever lived . . .

As though, even now, you are still standing outside the lounge door, terrified to enter the room your father is in, and yet unable to tear yourself away.

Instead: remain here for as long as you wish, letting the metal's coolness soothe you. Then, when you are ready, splash some water on your face – it feels good. Refreshing. Take a drink of cold water to rinse out your mouth. Slowly, slowly. There's no rush. Now dry your face.

Mary has gone, but no doubt she will be back in a short time with her patience, pity and understanding. Probably she will smile and reach for your hand – so be ready to take it, and to return the affectionate squeeze she will give. Meanwhile, run the taps for a few seconds to clear the sink – no damage done, in fact you're beginning to feel better already. Take a deep breath – she will be back at any moment.

It must have been raining earlier in the night, for when you open the window the room is filled with the scent of wet grass. You have been standing here for several minutes staring out into the darkness. The downstairs clock has just struck three. Do you realise how tightly you are gripping the wooden casement?

In four hours the rest of the family will be getting up. You will be with them: taking your place at breakfast, passing the toast and marmalade, pouring the tea, giving everyone your morning greeting and smile. You will know what to do then. But for the moment, however, there are only the darkness, the wooden casement, and the scent of wet grass – will that be enough until you are sitting at the kitchen table?

Once, when you were very young, you were playing on the floor of the living room when someone passed outside. You looked up.

'Is that me out there?' you asked your mother.

'What a silly question!' she replied, laughing. Then she picked you up and kissed you.

'A silly, silly question,' she repeated between more kisses and tickles. She leant towards you and then away with each kiss, with each repetition of 'silly, silly question'.

Over her shoulder, when she leant backwards, you could see the silhouette at the window. A man's. You were holding on to her dress. She was making you laugh;

the more you laughed the more she tickled and kissed you. 'Silly, silly boy,' she was saying as you kept trying to ask: 'Is that me?' but couldn't because of laughing. When the figure vanished, presumably to continue his walk along the street, you felt as if a part had been torn from inside you.

But the tickling and the kissing continued – forcing more laughter. You stretched out your hands to where the figure had been – and, in doing so, let go your mother's dress and almost fell from her arms. You sensed her fear instantly.

What do you feel now as you stand by the window holding desperately on to whatever's nearest to hand, staring straight ahead in terror? As though the texture of the wooden sill and the scent of the wet grass were parts of yourself already slipping from your grasp?

Until a moment ago you could hear the faint noise of traffic on the main road, a goods train clanking in the distance, a window being slammed shut further down the street—

Abruptly there is complete silence.

You have nothing to hold on to any more, not even your fear.

'What could you possibly know about love?' your father once demanded. Afterwards you longed to pull all the world's darkness into yourself to hide the unbearable shame he had thrust there. That was many years ago – yet now, as you stand alone at the window, you sense that same darkness, like mud, spreading everywhere around and inside you. Soon it will overwhelm you. Listen:

Yesterday you witnessed a stranger's death and felt it to be your own, in part. Tonight you stand here terrified that wherever you look you will see only yourself staring back.

You have reached a moment quiet enough to hear the sound of my voice: so now, as you stare out into the darkness, accept the comfort it can give you – and the love. The love.

11

The alarm clock – has stopped ringing. Lie still. Relax for a few moments before getting up. Let the sunlight colour in the room – that's its job, not yours. Relax. Kiss Mary. Say: good morning, Mary. And smile. This is the first day.

Getting dressed now. Talking with Mary: the day ahead, the weekend ahead. Another kiss – and already she's closed her eyes. If you want to, pause for several seconds to look at her. She is falling asleep again. Even in that short time she has fallen deeper into herself than you have ever gone, or ever imagined going.

Say her name, touching the back of her hand gently to waken her. Remind her it is time to get up.

You are trembling – listen to the sound of my voice. It is time to wash and go downstairs; to prepare the breakfast. To stand for a moment at the back door looking out across the lawn – the darkness, remember? The trembling will pass. Trust me. The ocean reaches from here to the far horizon – the present moment. No need to drink it dry. No need for anything.

Except for breakfast; for conversation and Clementi. No need for Courvoisier. If you're trembling – stir the tea and save energy! Trust me – it will pass. Every time it happens, it will pass. This is the first day.

A glance at the clock. A kiss and goodbye.

The walk to the station. I am with you. It is all right. Everything is. A day at the office, then home again. I will be with you. Trust me. The platform, *where the colour white flutters in front of the train to slow it down, then tangles in the wheels to bring it to a dead stop.*

It's over. Perhaps you will imagine this every time you stand here. But don't worry – it's all over. That will not happen to you. Trust me.

You are sitting in the carriage. It is crowded. There is a newspaper on your lap. It is hot in here, stifling. Although the windows are open you can hardly breathe. The carriage is already full, but more people clamber in at each stop. The distance between stops is getting longer. The people next to you press closer; those standing near you stand closer. You can feel the heat from them, the sweat, the mud. You stare at the page in front of you but cannot read.

More and people clamber in, pressing and jostling. You can smell them, taste them almost. You want to get to your feet and denounce them. For what? For the mud you see caking the sides of their eyes, the mud dried up in the corners of their mouths, the mud in the lines of their hands, under their nails, smeared under their clothes; the mud seeping out from their armpits and crotches. You are breathing mud.

As the train approaches each station, you think: 'This time I will get out,' but you remain in the corner, unable to rise from your seat; unable to say aloud, 'Excuse me, excuse me,' as you press your way through to the door. You will have to touch them, their heat, their body-slime. You will have to place your hand on their arms, on their shoulders; you will feel their mud-breath in your face as they turn to let you pass.

The train is slowing down now. Your stop. With the paper still in your hand you have stood up.

'Excuse me, excuse me,' you say. You are halfway between your seat and the door. Take your time – only a few feet to go. Not far.

'Excuse me, excuse me.' In a moment you will be in the fresh air: another step, then turn the handle – and out.

Is the train starting again? You can feel it shuddering into movement. You have grasped the door handle.

'Wait, wait!' you cry out as you throw open the door and stumble on to the platform – almost falling over. The train is quite stationary. Other passengers are still getting out of the carriages. The platform is crowded. You struggle to one side, to stand clear of the rush, and breathe deeply.

And more deeply.

This is the first day. One moment at a time. Stand still for one moment. Quietly. Quietly enough to hear the sound of my voice once more. You lost touch with me in the carriage when the mud began seeping in. In your panic you thrust me into the background as far as you could. Now the mud is rising inside you.

Gently, Morris. You cannot keep it down. Not by yourself. Gently, gently.

Go past the barrier and out of the station – one step at a time – across the car park and then the road. One step at a time. One moment, one step.

Trust me. The narrow lane leading to the main gate. I am with you. The mud is rising into your chest, choking you. It's all over the path, and you can hardly keep your feet any more as you slide from side to side, colliding with the metal railing, then with the wall.

But you must keep going. One step. Then grasp at the railing and hold on to it. Rest for a moment to gather your strength, letting the mud settle where it belongs – on the ocean floor, not here. Letting the colours of the grass, the flowers, the bricks and paving-stones return, and the path steady itself until even the slightest sunlight is held perfectly in place. Feel how delicately this moment is poised. Then, when you are ready, we'll go together into the next. Trust me.

Leave the railing and hold instead on to the sound of my voice. Listen: one step at a time.

One step towards the main gate. One step, another. One-step, two-step, another. Good.

Good. One moment, two, three, four – this is the first day. The main gate, the drive, the plate-glass doors, the lift, the open-plan, 'Good morning, good morning'.

Your office.

Pause, then: briefcase on the floor, coat on its peg. Pick up the briefcase to place it on the desk. Crossing the floor slowly. Then sit down. Relax.

Swivel and relax. For several moments. Your desk. The files Jan–Mar, April–June, the multicoloured graphs, the Mondrian. Relax.

Stand up. The window. The sky. For several moments stand and look at the sky. The ocean. The loading bay. For several moments. Good moments, bad moments.

Gently, Morris.

Gently. One Courvoisier – and the mud would settle

where it belongs. You could open the filing cabinet: one glass and one bottle for one drink. One drink to clear the mud.

But for you, *one* is no longer a number. For you, there cannot be one drink – just drink itself. From now on every day is the first day, and the first drink will be the final one. Trust me: flip the intercom instead.

'When you're ready, Carol.'

'Right away, sir.'

A glance outside at the clear blue sky.

Carol enters. She smiles at you.

'Lovely day today,' she remarks as she sits down.

You agree.

'Letters first?' she asks.

'Let us first what?' you enquire with a smile. Playful. A good moment.

She raises her eyebrows questioningly and then laughs. She has a sense of humour.

While you are in the middle of dictating a letter on projected sales trends you get up and walk over to the window. There are two lorries at the loading bay; you can see the foreman talking to crop-head. This is the first day. You continue speaking and Carol continues writing. There is a pause as you consider what to say next.

12

Saturday has barged into the room with shouting and whooping from Tom and Elise:

'Happy birthday, happy birthday!'

This is the second day – and still the first.

Thirty-five today, hooray. Halfway already.

Kisses, cards and presents. The whole family smiling and teasing. Breakfast in bed. Affection. You're trembling – it's with excitement, you tell them. Shaking and grinning – with excitement. But they must go in a minute to let you get dressed, you add. Hold on to my voice until they've gone.

Thirty-five years past – and thirty-five to come. And so – up, wash and brush your teeth. Hold on to the sound of my voice until the shaking, the trembling goes. It will. This is the second day – tomorrow you'll be rising from the dead!

Downstairs for the birthday celebrations.

A picnic. Surprise. A birthday surprise. Jokes, laughter and confusion. You have to get ready. Jacket and walking boots.

Ready?

You drive, they say.

Mary smiles and you smile back.

Birthday-boy behind the wheel.

Jokes, laughter and confusion.

Tom and Elise in the back seat waving bye-bye to

the house, then to the garden, the gate, the street, the city. You're taking them for a day in the country, for a picnic. A family outing.

Out on the open road. Then the motorway. Trembling inside. You'll soon have to stop, you tell them. For petrol, an oil check. The lanes on either side crisscross inside you – you can feel them cutting deep. Lacerating every sense and nerve to get to the sound of my voice – to silence me. You know Courvoisier would straighten them. A single glass. Trembling. You'll have to stop soon, you tell them. Gripping the wheel tighter. This is the second day – and still the first. From now on every day will be the first. The trembling will pass; the crisscross lanes will straighten by themselves. Trust me. Pull in for a few moments – for petrol and an oil check.

Back on the road, then a side road. A few miles. A parking place, then stop.

Begin the walk. A few steps. You're walking on the ocean now, letting it support you. Courage, Morris!

You've left the Thermos. Back to the car. Alone. Trembling. Listen to the sound of my voice. The second day, the twelfth hour. Every day, every hour is the first. But you are not alone now, nor will be again. The sun is colouring in the trees, the grass, the sky, the car you are leaning against. All that colour is flooding into you, its warmth saturating you – how could you possibly believe you are alone when you are part of all this? Pay attention, Morris – pay attention! The trembling has already passed – and you didn't even notice. Let's get the Thermos and get walking!

Trekker Trail Grade Five:

The Family Trail. Along a narrow path. Signposted. Kept clean. No ruins. No roads, lay-byes. No place for grief. An unspoiled nature park.

With the children hand-in-hand between you. Tom and Elise: three small steps to yours and two of Mary's. A picnic place. Stop. A rustic wooden table-stroke-bench unit. Mary gives out the sandwiches as you look round the hills and forests, pointing them out. Naming them sometimes. Further down there is a small bridge over a stream.

You begin: 'Did you know, you two, that if you walked over that bridge and kept walking straight on, then . . . ' You pause for a moment before continuing. 'If you kept going for long enough you would have to cross it again and again. As long as you kept walking,' you conclude, 'the same bridge.'

You have not explained it very well, and want to try again, but Tom and Elise have begun playing with the grass, blowing it edge-on to make it squeak.

'The very same bridge,' you tell them for a second time.

Later, a family walk: three-steps, two-steps. And back to the car. Time to head home.

'You drive', they say.

Mary smiles.

You smile back.

Birthday-boy behind the wheel.

Jokes, laughter and confusion.

Side road, main road, motorway, and nearly there.

Touching sixty with the accusations in the back seat, and Mary singing them a song:

'Down by the station early in the morning.

See the little puff-puff trains all in a row.'

And sixty-five. The suburbs: the three-lane keeps rising. *See the engine driver pull a little lever.* And rising, a flyover high above street-mud and shop-mud. Above rail tracks, goods yards and steel works. *And off we go.* Mary beside you singing:

'The owl and the pussy-cat went to sea.'

The accusations behind you:

'By the light of the moon, the moon.'

Silver-light in the fast lane: chromium bumpers, wing mirrors, radiators, headlamps and windscreens.

Seventy: the fast lane narrows two miles ahead. Silver-light diminished to white-road, white-verge, white-sky. The colour white all around you like silence, snow-silence. Your foot flat on the floor to return home before the light fails. Back from the picnic to the colour white where everything that has ever happened to you is still happening. The present moment. Criss-crossing to keep on course, tacking from side to side as the fast lane narrows. Each moment melting into the next like snow disappearing.

As though you have suddenly caught sight of your father straight ahead where the fast lane narrows.

As though at the same time he is behind you, shouting your name. You can hear him: his voice calling you from over thirty years ago when you jumped up suddenly at the picnic and began running downhill towards the main road, your arms stretched out in front. He is still coming after you to catch you, to hold you.

There is complete darkness on either side of the fast lane and mud everywhere: on the road, smeared across the windscreen, the dashboard. The steering wheel slithers under your hands. You grip it tighter.

You have almost reached your father, but he cannot seem to see you; you shout at him but he cannot seem to hear you. You drive at him, skidding from side to side in the mud. Behind you he is coming nearer. You sense his energy, his strength. His anger.

All at once you feel the road itself beginning to turn beneath the car's wheels, like a vast conveyor belt. It is your foot flat on the accelerator doing this: turning the road. A treadmill girdling the Earth. By driving full-speed at your father you are turning the Earth. At your back his anger has almost caught up with you.

The world is spinning so fast the car is almost out of control. To keep from careering into the darkness you drive faster and faster.

At the last moment your father seems to hear you; he begins as though to raise his arm in your direction – then abruptly he is gone.

It is only *now* that you are aware of Mary clutching on to you, her voice screaming at you to stop. There are tears running down your face as you release the accelerator and begin to slow down. When the car comes to a halt on the hard shoulder you are weeping uncontrollably.

Your tears – and mine.

The Sound of My Voice began as a short story. I can still remember sitting on the flat roof of my then girlfriend's place at the edge of Clapham Common in London, an A4 pad resting on my knee and writing, 'You are thirty-four years old and already two-thirds destroyed . . .'

Having already published two collections of poetry and one volume of short stories, I assumed this to be more of the same, as it were. Over the course of the following weeks, however, this particular short story kept getting longer and longer. As I'd saved some money from my recent stint as a Scottish–Canadian Exchange Writer, I was free to sit down every morning, A4 pad on my knees, and write and write. When my girlfriend and I separated, I drifted to Paris, Barcelona, Budapest and then to Edinburgh. Meanwhile every morning, A4 pad on my knee . . .

Thinking is over-rated, and in the initial stages of any creative work I find it an actual stumbling block. I am a fully-paid up member of the write-about-what-you-don't-know school. I write to explore, to discover – I don't do plans. Over thirty years and twenty books later I still get the same kick out of sitting down every morning . . . and letting my imagination carry me where it will.

The Sound of My Voice took several years to write and then rewrite. It is a short novel, a novella really, but was intermittently much longer. The chapters were not written in sequence and once a section was under way, I'd start on another and trust they would all fit together at some point. Only gradually did I begin to cotton on to what the novel was about. In fact, I'm not totally sure, even now. When no more sections were forthcoming, I began piecing what I had into some sort of order – a bit like doing a jigsaw, but without the boxtop picture to tell you what you're aiming for. After much cutting, editing and rearranging it seemed to make sense. It felt right.

As you may be a first-time reader I will avoid all spoilers – save only to say that the main character, Morris, is a fully-functioning alcoholic. He has it all – successful career, marriage, children, his own home. In society's terms, he has made it. Being Scottish I had drunk buckets of beer, wine and spirits as a teenager, then more or less stopped until Paris taught me the pleasures of wine with dinner – a lesson I still heed. Morris is different. Speaking in the second person, the voice talks him through his day in an attempt to keep him from destroying himself. The problem is, Morris has no wish to hear a word of what's being said – a not uncommon approach to life. The effects, of course, are catastrophic.

In 1987 the novel was published by Canongate and promptly disappeared. A Paladin paperback was published the following year – it also disappeared. Most unusually, I received a very kind letter from the publishers apologising for their lack of application.

I had poured my heart and soul into this novel, and its lack of readers coupled with the bewilderment of reviewers hit me harder than I probably realised at the time. Nevertheless I still continued to sit down every morning, A4 pad on my knee . . . I wandered here and there – Paris again, house-sitting in rural Spain, a commune in the Australian outback, the Far East – living very much hand-to-mouth. Finally I returned to Edinburgh and found, to everyone's surprise – my own, most of all – that I was going to get married. Regi came over from Switzerland (we had met and corresponded, met and corresponded) bringing a new kind of happiness into my life. Stability, too, sort of.

Then one day our phone rang. It was the *Village Voice* in New York telling me that Irvine Welsh had selected *The Sound of My Voice* as a Lost Classic and would I grant them permission to use quotes from the novel in his piece.

A few years after the novel had disappeared for the second time, a very small Scottish publisher had brought it out, after which it disappeared for a third time. But somehow, Irvine Welsh – whom I'd never met – had come across a copy. He saw it as a highly political novel, a polemic against Thatcherism and the consumer society. This had never occurred to me, but I saw it made complete sense. 'This book is one of the greatest pieces of fiction to come out of Britain in the 80s . . . Morris becomes a far more terrifying ghost at the feast of 80s consumerism than your stock McInerney-Amis character could ever be . . . ' Unfortunately there were no copies for sale in the States.

But things began to change. With Welsh's article as a

foreword, *The Sound of My Voice* was published yet again. This time by Pete Ayrton at Serpent's Tail, and it remained in print until very recently. Critics hailed the novel as a triumph; it began to be widely translated and to win prizes abroad, the French translation twice gaining a Best Foreign Novel award.

And now it is published for the fifth time. Fingers crossed, it is here to stay!

Ron Butlin, 2018